LOVE'S SWEET KISS

SASSY SEASONED SISTERS

SHERYL LISTER

Editor: Paulette Nunlee, 5 Star Proofing
Cover Design: Sherelle Green

For Nzinga Marshall Griffin
A Queen

ACKNOWLEDGMENTS

ACKNOWLEDGMENTS

My Heavenly Father, thank you for my life and for loving me better than I can love myself.

To my husband, Lance, you will always be my #1 hero! Twenty-six years and counting...

To my children, family and friends, thank you for your continued support. I appreciate and love you!

To my sister of the heart, Leslie Wright. Thank you for keeping me accountable. Love you to life!

To Karen Bracy, thank you for the brainstorming conversation. You rock, my sister!

Thank you to all the readers who have supported and encouraged me. I couldn't do this without you.

DEAR READER

Dear Reader ~

So many of you have expressed wanting to see more romances featuring "seasoned" folks and I am excited to introduce you to my new series featuring mature couples. These four ladies have it all, except that special man who can be the cherry on the top of a decadent sundae.

First up is Nzinga Carlyle and Byron Walker. I'm a sucker for second chances and, if anyone deserves to have one, these two do. And there's nothing like a man who knows what he wants. I hope you enjoy their journey to recapturing their love as much as I do!

Love & Blessings!
Sheryl

www.sheryllister.com
sheryllister@gmail.com

PROLOGUE

"*That* no good, *son-of-a—!*" Nzinga Carlyle clamped her jaws shut, jumped to her feet and paced the confines of the spacious office. When she hired her best friend, Donna Harper, who ran a private investigation firm, to find out anything to keep her soon-to-be ex-husband from dragging out their divorce any longer, she expected to find a few skeletons. But not this. She wanted to strangle him. "The lying, cheating bastard," she muttered.

"You okay, sis?"

She paused midstride and nodded, even though *okay* didn't come close to how she felt. Nzinga took a deep, calming breath and reclaimed her seat. "How did you find out about the account?" At the beginning of their twenty-five year marriage, Melvin Harris had convinced Nzinga to invest a thousand dollars in some stocks he'd assured her would be an easy way for them to build wealth. After checking them over, she agreed. A few months later, he had come to her and said the fund had gone belly up. Now, she'd just learned he had lied.

A wry grin curved Donna's lips. "Apparently, Melvin

cheated the man during some other scheme they'd cooked up later and Mr. Belker was more than happy to provide me with all the information I needed." She paused. "He also told me that Melvin never invested in the stock. Your thousand dollar check was the only one."

"*What?* He was supposed to be adding the same." With her being fresh out of med school and having student loans up to her neck, the money hadn't been easy to fork over. Nzinga had only met Mr. Belker the one time when she handed him her check and opened the account. She turned to her other friend and attorney, Valina Anderson. "So, what does that mean, Val?"

Valina crossed her legs, showing a red pump. "It means that every dime in that account belongs to you, since yours was the only deposit. Did you sign to have a joint account?"

"No. We were opening two accounts to double the money, he said," she added sarcastically.

"I know it's been over twenty years, but it would help if you still had the canceled check to prove it."

For the first time that morning, Nzinga smiled. "I have every check I've written since I opened my first checking account at eighteen." She leaned back in the chair. "Hopefully, this nightmare will finally be over."

There's more," Donna said.

She lifted a brow. Before she could comment, a soft knock sounded and Donna's assistant stuck her head in the door.

"Sorry to disturb you, Donna, but you said to let you know when Ms. Richardson arrived."

Donna nodded. "Thanks, Robin."

A moment later, the fourth member of the quartet of friends that had been together since sixth grade walked through the door. The hairs on the back of Nzinga's neck stood up. "What are you doing here, Max? Don't you have some babies to see?" Maxine worked as an occupational therapist.

Maxine leaned down and hugged Nzinga. "Donna asked me to come, so I rearranged my schedule."

Nzinga divided a wary glance between her friends. "What's going on?"

Donna released a deep sigh. "I just thought we should all be here." She slid a photograph across the table.

Her heart nearly stopped. She picked up the picture with shaky hands. "Are you telling me…?"

"I'm sorry, sis."

Anger the likes of which she had never experienced rose up so swiftly inside Nzinga, it took all her control to stay seated. If Melvin had been anywhere in the vicinity, she'd be needing bail money. When she and Val met with him and his attorney later this afternoon, it was going to take a Herculean effort not to jump across the table and knock the smug smile she knew he'd be wearing off his face. "How old is he?"

"Sixteen."

"So all that crap about being too busy to have kids was just that." She had wanted children and he'd professed the same, but as soon as the ink dried on their marriage certificate, it had never been the right time while he tried to climb the political ladder. She tossed the photo on the desk.

"He's been seeing the mother off and on over the years and has never missed a child support payment."

Max snorted. "That's because the jerk didn't want the city council or his constituents to know what an asshole he is."

"Along with a few others, apparently," Nzinga added. Their marriage had been steadily going downhill, but the day she happened upon him and some woman holding hands across a restaurant table was the day she ended it. Now, to add insult to injury, he had not only cheated, but also had a son.

Max grasped Nzinga's hand. "You know we've got your back."

She gave her friend a small smile. "I know, and I appreciate you all." Up to this point, she had tried to end this as amicably as possible. But she was done. She shifted her gaze to Val. "I want you to nail his trifling behind to the wall."

CHAPTER 1

*N*zinga dropped her purse on the bed and kicked off her shoes. The day had been a long one and she'd barely had time breathe. The office had been short one pediatrician and, rather than cancel the patients, she and the physician's assistant had seen them all. Since it was Friday, she would have the weekend to recover, and she couldn't think of a better way to unwind than to hang out with her girls. She went to the drawer and pulled out a pair of shorts and a tee. Although the calendar had just changed to June, the Sacramento temperatures had already climbed well into the eighties and nineties.

After a quick shower, she backed out of her driveway and made the thirty-minute drive from West Roseville to Donna's house in Natomas. When she got there, she saw that Max and Val had already arrived.

Donna answered the door within seconds after Nzinga rang the bell. "Hey, girl. Come on in." They shared a quick hug.

Nzinga followed her back to the family room. When she

entered, Val and Max stood and started cheering. She shook her head at their antics.

"How does it feel to be a free woman?" Max asked, bringing Nzinga in to a warm embrace.

"Better than I ever thought." She had received her divorce decree in the mail earlier in the week after almost two years of hassling with her ex. As a result, her three friends were hosting the celebration. "If it hadn't been for Donna finding out all that crap, I might still be trying to get out." She hugged Val. "It also helped that I had the best attorney in the country.

Val laughed. "I'd like to say you're lying, but…" She shrugged.

"Hey, if you don't brag on yourself, who will?" Max said.

"Amen!" they chorused.

Max snapped her fingers. "Speaking of crap, did you see Melvin's bid for governor fizzed out?"

Donna snorted. "Hard to run on a campaign of family when you have a baby mama and several side pieces." The women cracked up.

A few weeks ago, his photo had popped up on the news. Nzinga had changed the channel before the reporter could say one word. She could care less about him or his campaign. After the laughter subsided, they all took seats. She crossed her legs at the ankles. "What's for dinner? I'm starving. We had back-to-back patients today and I didn't finish lunch."

Max raised her hand. "Same here. I usually eat on the way to the next client's house, but they were all in the same vicinity and could only get in a couple of bites at a time." Maxine worked as a home-based pediatric occupational therapist, seeing clients birth to three years old. She often joked that she played for a living.

Donna smiled. "We're having Nzinga's favorite lasagna. I knew I wouldn't have time to make it, so I asked Monique to do it. She should be here in a few minutes." Monique was Donna's twenty-six year-old daughter and the goddaughter of the other three women. "The salad is done and the garlic bread won't take long. In the meantime, we need wine."

"You ain't said nothing but a word." Val jumped up and led the way to the kitchen. After all their glasses were filled, she lifted her glass. "To Nzinga. May she enjoy her newfound freedom."

"And may she find a sexy brother to help her get her freak on," Max added, which brought on another round of laughter.

"Crazy woman." They touched glasses and sipped. Nzinga shook her head. It had been so long, she probably wouldn't even remember *how* to get her freak on. That wasn't on her radar. For now, she just wanted to savor her newfound peace.

"Dinner's here!"

They all turned at the sound of Monique's voice as she entered the kitchen carrying a casserole dish.

Monique set the container on the stove. "I can't believe y'all started without me."

Donna snorted. "What do you mean started without you?"

She kissed her mother's cheek. "Aw, Mom. I am old enough to have wine." Turning, she greeted Nzinga with a strong hug. "Auntie N, congratulations on finally being rid of Mr. Meanie."

Nzinga chuckled. Growing up, Monique had always said Melvin was mean and grouchy. "Thanks, baby."

She repeated the gesture with Val and Max, then asked Max, "Have you talked to Dion?"

Pain crossed Max's features. "Not since Christmas." Max had been estranged from her twenty-three year-old son, Dion since divorcing his father six years ago. Max's ex had cheated on her and spun it to insinuate that she had been the one. Dion had taken his father's side and, outside of telling her son that she had been faithful to his father, had chosen not to give the then seventeen year-old the proof she had of his father's infidelity.

Monique rolled her eyes. "He is such a butthead. Do you want me to knock some sense into him?" The two had grown up together and Monique treated Dion like a younger brother.

Max smiled. "No. Hopefully, he'll come around on his own."

"Let me know if you change your mind."

"Okay, enough of that," Donna said as she slid a pan with the garlic bread into the oven. "The bread should be done in a few minutes, then we can eat. Monique, can you set the table for me?"

"Sure, Mom. I'll need an extra piece of that garlic bread as payment, though," she added with a little laugh as she went about the task.

Nzinga reached for the bowl of salad. "I'll take this to the dining room."

Val snatched it. "You just get to enjoy yourself tonight as the guest of honor, so sashay your behind on over to the table and sit." She waved a hand toward the dining room.

"Fine with me." She topped off her wine, spun on her heel and with an exaggerated sway of her hips, strutted out, leaving a trail of laughter from her friends. Nzinga didn't know what she'd do without them. They had seen each other through every trial and triumph and she couldn't have asked for better friends. She recalled the nights she cried over the demise of her marriage and how one or more of them had stayed with her for hours. Because Max had gone through the same thing, the two of them often consoled each other. A few minutes later, all the food was placed on the table and they started in on the meal. Nobody's lasagna recipe could top Donna's. "Monique, you have your mother's recipe down to a tee."

Smiling, Monique said, "Thanks. I watched her for years, trying to perfect it."

They ate in silence for a few minutes before Valina said, "Nzinga, you're free just in time for the reunion." Their thirty-fifth class reunion would take place in three weeks.

"*Free* being the key word. I'm enjoying my life the way it is and have no plans to change it. Besides, I am too old for games."

"Old? Who's old?" Max asked. "We're not old, just *seasoned*."

Nzinga lifted her glass in a mock toast. "Okay, I'll go with that." That statement brought on more laughter.

"I like it," Monique said. "Seasoned sisters. Wait, no, it's needs a little more pizzazz." She made a show of thinking, then grinned. "I've got it. *Sassy* seasoned sisters. Ooh, I should get you all T-shirts to wear to the class reunion. That would be so cool."

"Hey, I kind of like that."

"Max, don't encourage her." Donna stared at her daughter. "Don't you have a date with your fiancé or something?"

Monique smiled sweetly. "Nope. I made sure my evening was free because I didn't want to miss out on all this wisdom. I need to make sure I have all the do's and don'ts of this adult life."

"You're in the right place, baby." Max held up her wine. "To us sassy, seasoned sisters. May we dispense wisdom to youngsters everywhere."

"Amen!" Val said, touching her glass to Max's. They all followed suit. "Now, back to the reunion. I'm kind of looking forward to it. They're going to try to resurrect the jazz band."

"Are you going to play?" Donna asked.

"Yes, ma'am. I've already got the drum set up and have been dusting off the cobwebs. Lamont reached out to me on social media and said all twelve of us had agreed. The first practice is tomorrow."

Nzinga finished chewing her food and laughed. "I still remember the day you marched up to the band director and asked why there were only boys in the jazz band and told him you wanted to play drums."

Donna took up the story. "And the look on Desmond's face when you played him under the table during the drum-off for the position. He hated you until the day we graduated. Probably still does."

"I would've gone easy on him, but he tried to get in my face, talking about I needed to just worry about playing the bells." Val had played in the percussion section of the symphonic band, but had taken drum lessons from the age of seven and played with her older brothers. "Hmm…I wonder if he'll show up."

Nzinga eyed her. "Don't you get out there starting mess."

"I don't plan to start anything." She shrugged. "I was just wondering. Aside from him, I am looking forward to seeing a few people."

"And there are some who I'd rather not see," Max said. "Like creepy Calvin."

Nzinga frowned. "That boy was always trying to touch or kiss somebody."

"Well, if he tries it now, I will break him in half," Donna tossed out. The former police officer and Army veteran had a black belt in karate.

Max pointed her fork in Donna's direction. "You've got that right."

Monique's mouth fell open. "See, this is exactly why I stayed. I thought you guys were all sweet and now I find out that y'all are gangsta."

Donna rolled her eyes. "Girl, eat your food and hush."

She giggled and brought a forkful of lasagna to her mouth.

"At any rate, it should be fun," Nzinga said. "It looks like the committee planned it well." Friday night would be the opening activities with a casual dinner, Saturday had a family picnic during the day and formal dinner in the evening.

Max leaned back in her chair. "Nzinga, I wonder what happened to that guy you liked when we were freshmen."

Her brows knitted together. "What guy?"

"You know...his brother was in our biology class and was your partner on that big project we had to do," Val said. "What was his name?" She tapped her fingers on the table. "Wesley. That's it. But I can't remember his older brother's name."

"Byron," Nzinga said far softer than she intended. She hadn't thought of him in years. When her parents found out about them, their budding relationship was over before it got started. They had no intentions of allowing their fifteen-year-old daughter to date an eighteen-year-old *man* on his way to college in a few months. "I can't see why he would be there, since he's three years older than us."

"The family picnic, remember?" Max said with a sly smile. "Go ahead and admit it. You know you want to see what he looks like now."

"I'm not admitting anything. I'm sure he probably doesn't even remember me." However, she did think it would be nice to see him. Just to catch up, or at least that's what she told herself.

∾

"What's up, teach?" Byron Walker eased around a slow-moving car on the freeway.

Wesley Walker laughed. "Well if it isn't my lazy older brother."

"Don't hate. You're just mad you still have to punch the clock every morning. And I'm not the one who only works nine months out of the year. I gave Uncle Sam over thirty years of getting up at oh-dark-hundred, so I'm entitled to a little relaxation." He had retired from the military a year ago and was enjoying his life. The only thing that would have made it sweeter was if he had someone to enjoy it with.

"I need these three months after dealing with a bunch of high schoolers in the classroom. Anyway, what's up?"

"Just checking in and seeing if you're up for a visit."

"You're in town?"

"I will be in about an hour. I was in Lake Tahoe doing some fishing." Byron woke up Monday morning and decided to make the drive from Los Angeles to Lake Tahoe. He secured a hotel, left the next morning and spent three days just enjoying the scenery. He didn't catch any fish, however. His family lived in the Sacramento area and he hadn't seen his niece and nephew in months. Since his mother had been on his case about not staying in touch, he figured he could spend a few days visiting.

"Why didn't you tell me you were up this way?"

"I'm telling you now. Are you going to be around this weekend?"

"Actually, our class reunion starts tonight, so Loren and I are going. The kids are going to be out with friends, but tomorrow there's a family picnic, so you'll definitely have to come with us. How far away are you?"

"About forty minutes."

"Oh, well, come on over. The activities don't kick off until seven and it's only two now. You can get a chance to see the kids before they leave."

"Sounds good. See you in a few." Byron made the

remainder of the drive to Folsom with the smooth sounds of Boney James to keep him company. As soon as the door opened, his twenty-year-old niece, Anissa leaped into his arms.

"Uncle Byron!"

"Hey, baby girl," he said with a laugh. She didn't stand more than five feet, two inches, taking after her mother, and still exuded the same level energy she'd had as a little girl. He kissed her temple and set her on her feet. "How's college life?"

"Too much work. I'm so glad it's summer."

"Hi, Unc."

Byron did a fist bump with his seventeen-year-old nephew, Gabriel. "How's it going? Ready for senior year?"

Gabriel grinned. "Been ready."

He smiled at his brother. "What's up, little brother?" In addition to being three years older than Wesley, Byron also eclipsed his brother's six-two height by two inches and never missed an opportunity to point it out.

"Sleeping in," Wesley answered with a chuckle. "Retirement looks good on you. Come on in. You want something to eat or drink?"

"Nah, I'm good. Where's Loren?" He followed Wesley back to the family room and sat on the sofa.

He shook his head. "She had to get her hair done, nails done, feet done…and something else she said. With the list of things she rattled off, it'll be a miracle if she makes it back before it's time to leave."

Byron laughed.

"You're laughing, but you wouldn't be if you had a woman."

"Maybe, maybe not." Byron had a list of accomplishments, but the one thing he wished he could have added to the list was a family. Being in the military made it difficult to find a woman willing to deal with the multiple deployments. He'd come close a couple of times, but the relationships fizzled out before they could make it to the altar. Now, at almost fifty-seven, he'd just about given up on finding someone to share his life.

"How long are you planning to be here?"

"Probably until Monday or Tuesday, if you don't mind putting up with me."

"Not at all. Does Mom know you're in town?"

"No, and since you guys will be out tonight, I might head over there."

"You know Friday is her bingo night and she doesn't cancel going unless it's absolutely necessary."

"I know. I'll call her in a few minutes to see what she and Dad are doing tonight, but I'm not going to mention I'm here. I want to surprise them."

Wesley laughed. "Good luck with that."

They spent a few minutes catching up, then he called his parents. "Hey, Mom," he said when she answered.

"Byron. How are you, baby?"

"I'm good."

"You know we haven't seen you since Christmas and it's almost summer. With you being retired, I figured we'd get a chance to see you a little more often."

"Mom—"

"You might as well still be in the Army going on all those deployments."

He sighed and glared at Wesley, who was doubled over in his chair trying not to laugh out loud. When Naomi Walker got started, the only thing to do was sit and wait until she finished. "Mom, I promise I'll visit soon. I know this is your bingo night and you'll be leaving in a few minutes." She was usually out the door by four o'clock and his father left on his own for dinner.

"I'm not going tonight. Your Aunt Lee asked me to go with her to her doctor's appointment. I don't know why she needed to go on a Friday afternoon. She knows I have some-where to be," she fussed.

Byron chuckled. "I'm sure all that money will be there waiting on you next week."

"It better be because I've been on a winning streak." There was a pause on the line and muffled voices. "Your aunt is here. Don't make me have to send out a posse to find you."

"I won't, Mom. Tell Dad and Aunt Lee I said hello. Love you."

"Love you, too, honey."

He disconnected and shot another lethal glare at his brother. "Shut up, Wes. I don't want to hear one word."

Wesley burst out laughing. "Man, I wish you could've seen your face. I knew Mom was going to be all over you."

"Just tell me about the damn reunion."

It took a moment for him to stop laughing before he could talk. He finally composed himself enough to speak. "Like I said earlier, tonight is just a welcome dinner and tomorrow night is a formal one, which is why my wife has spent more money in the past week than she has all year."

Byron smiled. "She just wants to look good."

"No, she said she wants to make sure all those hussies who had a thing for me in high school know that they still don't have a chance."

It was his turn to laugh. "I love my sister-in-law. I just wish I could be there to see it play out."

"You can tomorrow if you join us for the family picnic. Speaking of women, I'm sure Darlene Butler would be happy to see you. She wanted you bad."

He made a face. "If she is, she'll be still wanting me until hell freezes over."

"Aw, come on, big brother. She might've changed by now."

"I doubt it." Their senior year, Byron had been the varsity basketball captain and Darlene the head cheerleader. Somehow, she had fixed in her mind that they should date and go to the prom together and had difficulties understanding he wasn't interested in doing either. The phrase "mean girl" came into existence because of her, and, back then, he'd had neither the time or inclination to deal with her foolishness. Still didn't.

"I thought you said you were trying to find a woman."

"I am, but she could never fit the bill." Yes, he continued to hold a slim hope of finding that one special person, but he wasn't desperate.

"What about my old biology lab partner, Nzinga Carlyle?"

Byron sat up straight. He had been fascinated by her back then, but with him being three years older, their parents had forbidden the relationship. He always wondered what would have happened had they been allowed to date. "I wouldn't mind catching up with her. She's probably married with a few kids like she wanted."

"Actually, she never had children. She was married to a guy on the city council, but I think they're divorced now."

"Hmm." This impromptu trip home might turn out better than he thought.

CHAPTER 2

"*J* can't believe all the people who showed up for this picnic," Nzinga said as she, Val, Donna and Max entered their high school campus. The grassy area was filled with blankets, beach chairs and canopy shades.

"Maybe we should've gotten here a little earlier. I hope we can find a spot." Val pointed. "Look, there's an area over to the right."

The women quickened their steps to claim the spot and made it just before another group got there. They spread out the large quilt, raised the easy up shade and set up their beach chairs.

"I don't know why we needed to bring chairs, since we have the quilt," Donna said.

Max stretched her legs out. "Because I sit on the floor all week. Today, I want to be an adult and sit on a chair."

"Yeah, well, nobody told you to get a job playing with babies. If you wanted to be an adult, you should have chosen a different field."

"Shut up, Miss Rambo."

Donna smiled. "Damn straight."

Nzinga shook her head. These women filled her life with so much joy.

"Love the shirts!" a guy passing called out.

True to her word, Monique had designed gray tees with the words "Sassy Seasoned Sisters" written in a fancy font. She'd also added rhinestones because, according to her, they needed a little bling.

"Well, if it isn't the four Musketeers."

They all stood to greet Lamont Johnson, the jazz band's keyboardist and leader.

"Y'all haven't aged a day in thirty-five years."

"Please," Nzinga said. "It's too early in the day for lying." He'd added a good fifty pounds to his former string bean frame, but his smile and easygoing manner hadn't changed.

"I came to get my girl. We're going to start the music in about thirty minutes."

Val retrieved her drumsticks from her bag and held them up. "I'm ready."

"You know Desmond's here, and when he heard the band was playing, he had the nerve to ask could he sit in as drummer."

Max folded her arms. "And when you told him Val was playing?"

Lamont laughed. "Stomped off just like he did the first time. I'll see you over there in a minute, Val. Good seeing you ladies."

"Same here," they chorused.

Because of where they were seated, they had a good view of the mock stage. Confident that their belongings would be safe, the four women slung their purses on their shoulders and went over to get something to drink.

"I should've known she'd be one of the first persons we'd see today," Max grumbled.

Nzinga glance up to see Cassandra Butler headed their

way with the same stuck-up crew she'd hung out with in high school. Cassandra had never liked her and Nzinga had no idea why. But she figured that was a long time ago and water under the bridge.

"Hey, Valina, Maxine and Donna," Cassandra said as soon as she approached. She looked Nzinga up and down with disdain. "I see y'all are still hanging out with trash."

Nzinga had been determined to take the high road, but this heifer was going to make her lose all sense of decorum. She gave Cassandra a false smile. "I see you still are trash."

The two women with Cassandra nearly choked on their drinks. Cassandra took a step.

She lifted a brow. *I know she's not.*

Cassandra opened her mouth, then closed it and stormed off, her two minions following.

"I'm glad she decided not to cause a scene," Val said. "Maybe she's grown up some."

Max shook her head. "Nah, sis, that was a business decision. She remembered what happened the last time she tried to get in Nzinga's face."

Donna smiled. "Yeah, girl. She might still think she's all that, but she's not stupid."

Nzinga didn't care about the reason, she just hoped the woman kept her distance for the remainder of the weekend. In their freshman year of high school, Cassandra had made a habit of harassing Nzinga almost daily for a week. Nzinga grew tired of trying to be tactful and the next time Cassandra walked up, intending to start trouble, Nzinga dropped her with one punch, then walked away. "I'm not going to spend my time thinking about that crazy woman. We came here to enjoy ourselves, so let's do it." After getting bottles of tea, she, Donna and Max headed back to their spot, while Val went to join the band.

The band took them back, playing everything from

smooth jazz, to the R&B songs that had been popular during that time—"Cutie Pie" by One Way, "Forget Me Nots" by Patrice Rushen and "Take Your Time" by The S.O.S. Band— and had everyone on their feet dancing.

"Desmond doesn't look too happy," Donna said with a little laugh, pointing to where he stood near the stage glaring, no doubt, at Val as she flipped her sticks and never missed a beat.

Nzinga playfully bumped her shoulder. "I wouldn't either, if a *girl* could wipe the floor with me on the drums."

They launched into Earth, Wind and Fire's Shining Star and Max threw her hands in the air. "*Yaassss!* This is my *jam!*"

Apparently, that feeling was shared by everyone gathered —young and old—if the sheer volume of shouts that went up were any indication. At the end of the song, the audience all joined in to sing the final refrain acapella.

Nzinga clapped along with the crowd when it was over. "Oh, my goodness. They were fabulous. I didn't realize Val had kept up with her playing."

"Neither did I," Max said. "Girlfriend needs to put her pumps to the side and take this show on the road."

"No lie."

Donna elbowed Nzinga. "Girl, look who's coming this way."

She turned in the direction Donna gestured and saw Wesley Walker approaching with a man who she would recognize anywhere. Her heart started pounding just like it did the first time she'd seen him at their house when she and Wesley were working on a biology project. Byron stood six feet, four inches, had smooth, dark caramel skin and muscles for days. But it was his light brown eyes that had totally captivated her. And every other girl at the school. The way he stared at her now still had her mesmerized.

Max scooted close to her and whispered, "Honey, that

man is even finer than he was then. I sure hope he's single, especially since he can't seem to take his eyes off you. And that salt and pepper beard...*sexy!*" She cleared her throat and opened her arms. "Wesley Walker, the smartest guy in the world. How are you?"

Wesley laughed and embraced Max. "I don't know about that, but I'm good." He repeated the gesture with the other women, including Val, who'd just joined them. Then he placed his arm around a woman. "This is my beautiful wife, Loren."

Loren smiled easily and reached out to shake each of their hands. "I've heard a lot about you all over the years."

They all greeted Loren and Nzinga said, "I hope nothing bad."

"Not about you ladies, but I have heard a few stories about some others," she said conspiratorially.

Wesley chuckled. "Don't get her started." He introduced his two children. "I don't know if you all remember my brother, Byron. Lucky him, he came up for a visit just in time to attend this shindig."

"Who could forget the varsity basketball captain who led our team to the first championship in over a decade?" Donna said.

Byron smiled. "It's nice to see you ladies again." He turned to Nzinga and grasped her hand. "It's been a long time, Nzinga."

"Yes, it has." She ignored the knowing looks on her friends' faces. Nzinga thought herself far past the age of being affected by a man. But the mere touch of Byron's hand on hers made her pulse skip and had her heart beating at a pace that had to be dangerous. She couldn't remember the last time any man made her feel this way.

∾

Byron stared at Nzinga for a full minute, unable to take his eyes off her. He'd recognized her the moment he spotted her with the group of friends he remembered had always been together. The pretty young girl who had stolen his heart without even trying had grown into a gorgeous woman with the regal bearing of a queen. With her coffee with cream skin and trim, toned arms and legs, one would never guess she was in her fifties. He finally found his voice. "How've you been?"

"Doing well," Nzinga answered with a smile. "And you?"

"I'm good." Better than good, now that he'd seen her.

"Wesley mentioned you're visiting. How long are you planning to be in town?"

He nodded. "I came up from LA and I'll probably be here for a couple of weeks." Wesley swung his shocked gaze in Byron's direction and Byron ignored him. He glanced down at Nzinga's ring finger and saw it was indeed empty. "Maybe we can catch up on old times while I'm here, if you're not too busy."

"That would be nice."

Before he could comment he heard someone calling his name and spun around.

"Byron Walker? Big B, I thought that was you, man!"

"Grant. Hey." The man pumped Byron's hand so hard he thought it would fall off. For the life of him, he couldn't understand why Grant acted like they had been best friends, when they'd never spoken more than two words to each other during their high school years.

"I want you to meet my girl. She's over there." Grant pointed at a group standing several feet away.

Byron really didn't want to leave. He would rather talk to Nzinga, but excused himself and followed Grant. When the man said he wanted Byron to meet his girl, Byron thought he'd meant it in an affectionate way. Apparently, he'd meant it literally. The smiling woman who draped herself all over Grant couldn't have been much older than Byron's niece. Grant had always considered himself a ladies man.

"Nice to meet you, Byron. My baby said you guys played basketball together and you helped him take the team to the championship."

His brow lifted. "We did and, as the team captain, I think I had a little more to do with the team winning." Byron had made first team all-state the three years he played varsity and had a scoring record that still stood after almost forty years. Grant had only been a starting player halfway through their senior year because one of the guards got hurt. Byron couldn't recall one game where the man had scored more than ten points.

Grant patted her on the butt and chuckled nervously. "Now, sweetheart, that's not exactly what I said. Byron, I know you want to get back to your family. I just wanted you to meet Honey. It was good to see you."

"Yeah, I do need to get back. See you around." *I guess some things never change.* He was disappointed to find Nzinga gone when he returned. He scanned the area, spotted his brother and headed in that direction. Halfway there, the one person he had been trying to avoid came toward him. Byron groaned inwardly. Darlene Butler. She had on a skimpy outfit that revealed more than it covered and enough makeup for two clowns. Nzinga, on the other hand, had worn a pair of nice shorts that accentuated her curvy hips and stopped a few inches above her knees and a top that gave a hint of cleavage and left the rest to one's imagination. Classy.

"Oh, my goodness! Byron, it's so good to see you." Darlene grabbed him up in a crushing hug.

Byron quickly untangled himself and took a step back.

The cloying perfume she wore almost made him choke. "How are you, Darlene?"

"I'd be much better if you told me you're still single," she said with a coy smile.

"Sorry." He didn't lie exactly. "Have a good time." He pivoted on his heel and hurried across the campus to where his family sat eating.

"Problems?" Wesley asked.

"Don't ask."

"She's been watching you since we got here, probably waiting to make her move."

"I only knew who she was because I heard someone call her name earlier and I made sure to stay out of her line of sight."

Wesley grinned. "My guess is she was hoping to make you husband number three...or is it four?"

He shot his brother a dark look.

"Man, I can't believe how much drama old people have," Gabriel said, shaking his head and biting into a fried chicken wing.

Loren laughed. "Since you were a little busy, I fixed you a plate."

"Thanks." Byron lowered himself to the blanket and accepted the offering.

"I thought you were leaving in a couple of days, not a couple of *weeks*," Wesley said casually as he took a sip of his Coke.

He froze with the fork halfway to his mouth.

Loren playfully swatted Wesley on the arm. "Leave your brother alone, Wes." She turned to Byron. "Nzinga is a beautiful woman and she seems really nice. You're welcome to stay as long as you need."

"Thanks, sis."

"It's about time you found a woman to help you get your

groove on," she added with a wink.

Byron choked on the piece of chicken he had just swallowed. Coughing, he stared at Loren.

Anissa patted him on the back. "Are you alright, Unc?"

"Fine," he croaked, still trying to clear his throat.

"Was she your girlfriend back in the day?"

"No."

"The way you were looking at her said you wished she was," she said with a giggle.

He reached over and tugged on her ponytail. "Stay out of grown folks business." He managed to get through the meal without further comments. As soon as he finished, he searched for Nzinga.

"She's sitting in the same spot on the right side of the field." When Byron met Wesley's gaze, Wesley shrugged. "Just trying to be helpful."

"Thanks. I'll be back." He disposed of his plate and soda can, then made his way over to where Nzinga sat with her friends. She laughed at something and the sound hit him squarely in the chest. "Ladies."

"You coming to chat with our girl?" Max asked.

"If you don't mind."

"We don't," the three women said.

Byron smiled.

An embarrassed expression crossed Nzinga's face. "I can't stand y'all."

Max waved Nzinga off. "Aw, girl, you know you love us. Go on and enjoy yourself."

Nzinga stood. "Don't pay them any attention."

"Oh, you should invite him to be your guest at the dinner tonight. That way, you'll have more time to catch up, since the picnic is almost over."

He wanted to hug Max. She tossed him a wink and he nodded in acknowledgement. He and Nzinga started a slow stroll, neither of them speaking for the first couple of minutes. He felt like an awkward teen on his first date.

"Don't know why I'm feeling a little nervous," she said.

He laughed softly. "Thank goodness. I thought I was the only one." They shared a smile.

"So, how did you get to LA?"

"The Army. I retired last year after thirty-five years. For my last two assignments, I served as a commander with defense contracts, so I had a nice office."

"That's quite an accomplishment. I assume you were an officer."

"Colonel. What about you? I remember you talking about going to med school."

"I did and have a pediatric practice with another doctor."

His eyes widened. "Are you kidding me? That is fabulous. So I should be calling you Dr.—" He didn't even know her last name.

"Carlyle. I kept my maiden name for professional purposes. It turned out to be a good decision," Nzinga added softly.

"I'm sorry." The hurt in her voice moved him in a way he hadn't expected and it took everything in him not to wrap his arms around her.

"Don't be. It was for the best."

They fell silent as they continued their leisurely stroll.

"Is there a special lady in your life?"

"No. I never married."

Her shocked gaze flew to his. "You're kidding me, right? What was wrong with all those women?"

A smile curved his lips. "Military life isn't for everyone, and how do you know I wasn't the problem?" He'd had two long-term relationships he thought would end in marriage, but both fizzled out after a year.

"In high school, you were sweet, considerate and a gentleman, and from what I've seen today, you haven't changed, so it must've been them."

He didn't reply, but her words made him stand a little taller.

"I guess the picnic's over."

Byron noticed that people had started packing up, but he didn't want his time with Nzinga to end. "I guess so." He didn't even have his car or know if she'd driven, so he couldn't offer to take her home. Their footsteps took them in the direction of where her friends stood, gathering their belongings. Byron really wanted to ask about the dinner and dance that evening, but didn't want to come on too strong. "I've enjoyed talking to you."

"Same here." Nzinga stopped. "I don't know what your plans are for the evening, but I'd like to continue our conversation. Would you like to be my guest for tonight's dinner?"

Inside, he was doing a happy dance, but managed to keep his cool. "I'd love to. Wes mentioned the hotel where the party will be held." He whipped out his cell and opened the contacts. "Can you input your address and phone number?"

Smiling, she complied and handed the phone back. "It starts at seven."

"Then I'll pick you up at six-thirty."

"I'll be waiting."

Byron said goodbye to her friends. "See you later, Nzinga." He hadn't been this excited about a date in a long time, if ever. It occurred to him that he didn't have anything in the way of formal wear with him. He took a quick peek at his watch. He had three hours and he needed to go shopping.

CHAPTER 3

*N*zinga endured good-natured teasing all the way home. Instead of driving their own cars, they'd met at Max's and she drove her SUV.

Max glanced in the rearview mirror. "I wish you could've seen the smiles on both your faces. It was so cute."

"I know, right," Val said. "And you guys look really good together. It's really a shame you didn't have a chance to date back then."

"I don't know about all that." Although, Nzinga couldn't deny how happy she had been talking with Byron.

Donna shifted in her seat to face Nzinga. "Did you ever think about what would've happened or where you'd be if you'd ended up with him, instead of Melvin?"

"I thought about it when we talked briefly after graduation, but that's all." She stared out the window. Byron had come home for Wesley's graduation and they'd snuck off for a few minutes. The memory of their kiss rushed back, along with the sadness she had felt, knowing they still wouldn't have a chance to be together. They had gotten interrupted and never had a chance to exchange information. She was headed to Howard University and he, back to UCLA. Nzinga had cried for weeks just as she had in ninth grade, her heart broken all over again. Once she started college, she poured everything into her studies. Max's voice drew her back into the conversation.

"Has he been married?"

"He said he'd never married." A fact that still boggled her mind.

"That's because he was waiting for you," she said.

"Max, the man probably hadn't thought about me until today. It's been three and a half decades since I've seen him and—"

"And that spark is still alive and kicking," Donna finished. "When Byron left, he said see you later, so I'm assuming you invited him tonight."

"Yes. I figured it would be nice to catch up." The way he'd stared at her earlier was the same as when they were younger and the thought of spending the evening with him made her uncharacteristically nervous. Nzinga didn't understand why. It wasn't as if they were strangers. Then again, it had been a long time and they had changed. She certainly had, particularly when it came to men. No longer was she the wide-eyed trusting young woman who fell for any smooth-talking man.

Val smiled. "You guys will be catching up, alright. I'll bet you anything there will be some kissing involved by the end of the night."

"Agreed," Max said. "At least one of us needs to get some practice in. Hell, it's been so long since I've had a good kiss, I'm trying to remember what it feels like."

Val laughed. "Girl, for real!"

"I'm good," Donna said. "I don't need the headache, but Nzinga, I think you should take the plunge." Of the four friends, Donna harbored the most hurt. They all knew it had a lot to do with her family, but outside of a few details, Donna hadn't been forthcoming with much information.

"Whatever." But Nzinga was smiling. When she got home, she went straight to her closet. The dress she had planned to wear, somehow, didn't fit the bill now. She chuckled. A date. Nzinga let out a squeal and did a little hip swerve, then searched for something date worthy.

She went through and discarded dress after dress, pausing at a navy sleeveless, scoop neck floor-length dress with a sheer back, ruched waist and a side slit that stopped a few inches above the knee. Holding it against her, she smiled. She'd gained a few pounds and her stomach wasn't as flat as she liked, but for a fifty-three-year-old woman, Nzinga thought she looked pretty good.

After showering and relaxing for a while, Nzinga got dressed. Instead of wearing her hair pulled back in her typical bun, she opted to leave it down, part it off center and flat iron the shoulder-length strands so that they hung in a mid-length bob. She applied makeup and spritzed on her favorite perfume, then sat on the edge of the bed to strap on her silver sandals. She stood before the mirror, turning one way, then another, pleased with the way the dress skimmed her curves. The doorbell rang and the butterflies returned full force. Taking a deep, calming breath, she stood and made her way to the front.

Anything Nzinga had planned to say died in her throat the moment she opened the door. Byron had always been good-looking, but with his ramrod-straight posture, commanding height and wearing a navy suit and pale gray shirt that had to have been tailored just for him, the man gave new meaning to *fine*. In her three-and-a-half-inch heels, he still towered over her by a good half a foot. It took her a moment to realize he was staring at her the same way.

Finally, she found her voice. "Please, come in." She moved aside for him to enter.

Bryon stepped inside, towering over her. He handed her a long-stemmed red rose. "You look beautiful."

"Thank you." He brushed a kiss over her cheek and her pulse skipped. He smelled so good.

"I didn't think to ask what you were wearing, but I'm glad I got the memo."

They both burst out laughing. "Yes, you did. Let me get my purse and we can leave." Once that had been accomplished, she followed him out to a late model Acura SUV that looked to be freshly washed and waxed. She endured the heat of his body again as he held the door open for her. When he went around to the driver's side, Nzinga took a moment to compose herself. It wasn't like she hadn't dated since her divorce. *True, but none of those men had ever held your heart, either,* an inner voice said.

He started the car and drove off. "Is the temperature okay?"

"Fine." The late June temperatures had climbed into the nineties and, even though early evening, the heat hadn't abated.

"Tell me about your practice."

Shifting in her seat, she told him how she and another doctor had worked in a larger practice and had issues with the way patient care was being carried out. "Instead of us treating the kids based on their individual concerns, they had this cookie cutter profit-based system. I didn't spend all those years in med school for that kind of nonsense."

Byron slanted her an amused gaze. "It seems like medical care is going that way everywhere. It takes forever to get an appointment, then you're in and out in five minutes, most times with a prescription."

"Exactly. Over lunch one day, Henry asked me what I

thought about him and I starting our own practice. It took us another year to get everything together, but ten years later, we're still standing strong."

"That took a lot of guts and I wish I could've been here to cheer you on. I know it's a little late, but congratulations."

"Thank you." His response was so different from Melvin's. Her ex couldn't understand why she would choose to leave a lucrative practice for a startup. They had argued about it for a solid month. He hadn't even planned to show up to the ribbon cutting until someone from his office caught wind of it and thought it would be a good photo op. But she'd nixed that idea. Nzinga had no intentions of turning their hard work into a circus. They were there for the children and their families. Period. The old anger came back, but she pushed it and the memory aside. Today was a new day and she didn't ever have to deal with Melvin and his shenanigans again. She changed the subject. "Did you enjoy military life?"

"Enjoy is a strong word," he said with a chuckle. "I initially planned to do four years, see the world a bit, then get out and snag a job as a materials engineer. But after completing officer candidate school, I decided to make it a career."

"Any regrets?"

"Just not having the family I always wanted."

She had the same regret. The conversation tapered off as they arrived at the hotel.

Byron parked in the valet lane, came around to help Nzinga out of the car and handed off his key to one of the young men, exchanging it for a ticket. He placed his hand in small of her back and guided her inside. "I didn't think to ask Wes the name of the room."

"It's the Grand Ballroom, but I'm sure if we just follow all these people and the music, we'll find it."

"And that sign right there would probably help, too." He grinned and extended his arm. "Shall we?"

She returned his smile and placed her hand in his arm and they started in that direction. When they entered the ballroom, she could swear every eye in the place turned their way. Nzinga met the smiling faces of her girls and, Max with her outrageous self, had her phone up snapping pictures. A few tables away, Cassandra and her sister, Darlene glared, but Nzinga didn't pay them any attention.

"Looks like your friends saved some seats."

"Are you okay sitting with them?"

"As long as I'm sitting where you are, I'm good." He urged her forward.

Oo-kay. She greeted her friends. "Y'all look so good."

Val, sitting in the seat next to the one Nzinga chose leaned over and hugged Nzinga. "So do you." Then for her ears only, she said, "You're going to be the envy of every woman in this room. Damn, he looks good."

Nzinga chuckled. "Hush."

"Ladies, you look lovely," Byron said.

"Thanks," they chorused.

Lamont and two other classmates had joined them and laughter and conversation flowed around the table all through the dinner hour.

When the music started, Lamont stood. "Come on, Val. Let's show these folks how it's done."

Already dancing to the beat, Valina hopped up and followed him to the dance floor. A guy who had been infatuated with Max in high school came and claimed her.

Byron held out his hand. "Dance with me?"

"Of course." Nzinga let him lead her out and they danced to song after song. When it came time to do the electric slide and the Wobble, they lined up with the other people and never missed a beat. It was the most fun she'd had in a long time. After what seemed like forever, she said, "Okay, this old body needs a break." She fanned herself.

"My body is older than yours and I know I'm going to pay for it in the morning. But it will be worth every ache," Byron added with a laugh.

"Amen." They went to the bar and ordered glasses of wine. As they sipped, she watched the people still dancing. A few of them seemed to have no idea what rhythm meant, but they were having fun and that's all that mattered. She turned and found Byron staring at her intently. "What is it?"

For a moment, he said nothing. "I was just thinking about my prom and how I had been looking forward to dancing with you. When your parents wouldn't let you go with me..." His voice trailed off.

Nzinga understood. She later found out he'd gone alone and that hurt her, as well. They'd both missed out on that special moment in time. Without thinking, she reached up and touched his cheek. "I know. We can't go back, so let's enjoy ourselves tonight."

The music changed to a ballad. Byron took their glasses, set them on the table behind them and escorted her to the dance floor once again. "You're right, and I am enjoying myself."

When he slid an arm around her waist, pulled her close and moved in time with the sultry beat, she almost melted.

"I always wondered what it would feel like to hold you in my arms and it's even better than I imagined."

Oh, mercy. She went weak. Her legs felt like jelly and had he not been holding her, Nzinga would have slid to the floor. She managed to finish the song without embarrassing herself, but with the way his hands moved subtly over her body, whether she made it through the rest of the night remained to be seen.

Byron walked Nzinga to her door, reluctant to end the evening. He never imagined how much he would enjoy her company. They'd laughed and danced the night away. He hadn't meant to mention the prom. As she'd said, they couldn't change the past, but he'd always been a straightforward person and tended to say what was on his mind.

Nzinga unlocked the door. "Would you like to come in?"

"Just for a minute." He followed her in. She sat in the nearest chair and removed her shoes. The sound of relief she made sent heat straight to his groin. He'd been celibate by choice for the past year and a half and being with her today reminded him of that fact.

She let out another sigh of relief and stood. "That's better. Can I get you something to drink?"

"No, thanks. I'm not going to stay." Byron closed the distance between them. "Thank you for inviting me to share your evening. I really enjoyed myself."

Smiling, she said, "So did I. It was good to see you again."

"Could we have dinner sometime this week?" He wanted to have that dinner tomorrow, but he owed his parents a visit. Besides, he needed a few days to contemplate the unexpected emotions swirling around in his gut.

"I'd like that."

"I'll give you a call and you can tell me which day works best for you." He tried to think of something else to say to delay his departure, but in the end decided it was best that he leave. It was nearly one in the morning. She walked him to the door.

"Thanks again for being such a great date."

He nodded. Before he could stop himself, he bent and kissed her softly. The moment their lips touched, it transported him back to the stolen kiss they'd shared when he came home for Wesley's graduation. Then and now, the kiss hadn't lasted long enough, but he figured he needed to back off. "I'm…do I need to apologize?"

"No."

Byron smiled faintly. "Goodnight, Nzinga."

"Goodnight. Drive safely."

He gave her hand a gentle squeeze and sauntered down the driveway to his car. It took almost forty-five minutes to get back to his brother's house. He smiled, thinking about Loren slipping the house key in his hands and whispering, "Just in case you and Nzinga need a little more time." The house was dark and quiet and he silently made his way to the first floor guest room. After a quick shower, he slid between the crisp, cool sheets. He should be exhausted, but his mind raced with thoughts of his evening and it took a long time for him to fall asleep.

Byron was used to rising early and now that he'd retired, sleeping in translated to seven-thirty or eight. However, he stumbled out of bed at ten after only four hours of sleep. He had lain awake until the sun started its ascent into the sky. When he walked into the kitchen, Wesley was sitting at the bar drinking coffee and reading the newspaper.

"Long night, big brother?"

"Had a hard time falling asleep."

Wesley folded the paper and placed it next to him. "Thinking about Nzinga?"

He and Wesley had always shared a close relationship, so he had no problem telling the truth. "Yes. Didn't expect all the old feelings to come back." He grabbed a cup from the cabinet, poured himself a cup of the dark brew and slid onto a barstool opposite his brother.

He studied Byron a long moment. "Is that a good or bad thing?"

"I don't know, but I'd like to say it's good. She's the same sweet person I remember, and we had a great time together."

"Those intense looks between you two had more than a few women jealous, according to Loren. Of course, she thought you guys were cute," he added with a little laugh. "I take it you plan to see her again, since you decided to extend your stay."

Byron added a teaspoon of sugar to his coffee, stirred and took a sip before answering. "I invited her to dinner sometime this week."

"Are you still going over to Mom and Dad's today?"

He nodded. "This afternoon. Is everybody still sleep?"

"The kids are, but Loren is up and reading. They'll all be down for breakfast within the next hour."

"I'll help you cook. It's been a while since we've prepared breakfast together." Their family was big on eating together whenever possible and as teens, the two of them would do Sunday brunch. Grinning, they decided on a menu and got to work. By the time everyone emerged from their rooms, the bar was lined with scrambled eggs, bacon, sausage, potatoes with onions and bell peppers, and biscuits.

Loren kissed Byron on the cheek. "Oh, this looks so good. You need to come visit more often."

Byron laughed. After everyone filled plates, they sat at the dining room table. As the laughter and teasing began, he felt a touch of envy seeing and listening to the way Wesley, Loren and the kids interacted. He missed this.

"Can we do this every week?" Gabriel asked.

"If you plan to help, sure," Wesley said.

"Okay. I'm down with that."

It didn't take long for all the plates to be empty. Loren and the kids cleaned up, while Byron and Wesley retreated to the family room to watch the baseball game, but his mind strayed to Nzinga and what she might be doing. Byron had wanted to call her first thing this morning, but resisted. He couldn't remember the last time he had been this anxious to talk to a woman. His recent dating life had consisted more of group outings than individual date nights. He'd been looking for a special someone, but had yet to find her. Once again, Nzinga's face floated across his mind's eye. Wesley's voice filtered through his musings. "What did you say?"

"I said, maybe you should just give in and call her."

"I don't want to come on too strong, especially after last night."

Wesley sat up. "What happened last night? Did you two sleep together?"

He shot his brother a lethal glare. "Not that it's any of your business, but I'm fifty-six, not *twenty-six*, Wes. Give me a little credit. No, I kissed her goodnight. Nothing too deep, just soft and sweet." He scrubbed a hand down his face. "It wasn't anything I planned, though. We were standing there and I was remembering how much I liked her in high school." A more honest assessment would be that he'd been in love with her from a distance. It had taken until his second year of college before he ventured out on a date.

"You know they say you never really get over your first love, and before you try to deny it, Nzinga *is* the first girl you fell in love with." Wesley paused. "I was there and I remember how torn up you were about her. Maybe this will be a second chance for both of you."

"I don't know. Maybe. It could be these are just residual feelings from back then."

"Only time will tell."

"Yeah." Byron stood. "I'm going over to Mom and Dad's. Be back in a while."

On the drive, he thought more about his conversation with Wes. Could this be their second chance? They were no longer teens barely moving into adulthood. They'd both had life experiences that shaped who they had become and, after being alone his entire life, he probably had developed more than a few habits of a bachelor.

When he drove up to his parent's house, a smile creased his face as he recalled his mother's admonishment about him needing to visit more often. She was right. His parents had reached their eighties and, although, neither of them had any serious health issues outside of the normal ones associated with aging, he vowed to make more frequent trips. He rang the doorbell and chuckled at the stunned look on his mother's face when she opened the door. With her nearly wrinkle-free dark brown face and trim, petite body, Naomi Walker could pass for someone twenty years younger.

"Byron! What are you doing here?"

He shook his head. "Weren't you just fussing at me two days ago about visiting? Now, you're asking me why I'm here."

She swatted him on his arm. "You know what I mean." She glanced around him. "You're alone?"

"Of course."

She grunted. "I thought you were really going to surprise me."

Byron's brow lifted. "Mom, what are you talking about, and are you going to make me stand on the porch in this heat all afternoon?" She backed up and held the door open, and he kissed her cheek.

"Since I'm not getting any more grandchildren, I figured you were showing up to tell me you're getting married. I love Loren, but having another daughter-in-law would make everything complete."

He laughed. "Sorry. No fiancée and I'm not even dating anyone." Nzinga's face flitted across his mind. *Not yet, anyway.* He followed her to the family room.

Turning back, she scowled at him. "You're not getting any

younger. How hard is it to find a nice young lady, especially now that you're in one place?"

A wide grin split his father's face when Byron entered the room and he slowly rose to his feet. "Hey, son." He engulfed Byron in a strong hug. "Your mama couldn't even let you get in the door before she started nagging you, huh?" he asked with a chuckle.

"Hi, Dad. Nope." He stared into the face that mirrored his own. He and Byron, Sr. shared the same height, but his father had lost a few pounds since Byron had seen him at Christmas.

"Have a seat. How long have you been here?"

He sat on the sofa and stretched out his long legs. "I got in late Friday afternoon and had planned to come over yesterday, but I ended up going to Wes's class reunion family picnic."

"Oh, yes, he mentioned that," his mother said, reclining her chair. "Did you see anyone from your class?"

"A few people." And most of them he could have gone without seeing. He'd missed his last reunion due to work and hadn't lost any sleep over it.

"Was that little fast girl that used to call here every day and drop over with those lame excuses there? Darlene something or other." Naomi had never liked Darlene.

"I saw her briefly." She still hadn't changed. He had spotted her at the dinner last night and if looks could kill, he would have dropped dead then and there. Fortunately for him, she'd had the good sense to keep her distance. "Do you remember Wesley's lab and study partner?" She had been a fixture in their house.

She smiled. "Nzinga Carlyle. She was such a lovely girl and smart as a whip. I wonder what she's doing now. Seems like I remember seeing something years ago about her being married to someone on the city council."

"She's a pediatrician and has a private .practice with another doctor." And the lovely girl was now a drop-dead gorgeous woman. Byron glanced up to see both his parents staring at him. "What?"

"Something you want to tell us, son?" his father asked.

"No, why?"

"The shine in your eye when you mentioned Nzinga was hard to miss. And I remember how hard it was on you when her parents said she was too young for you."

Byron had no idea how to explain what he felt, so he kept quiet.

His mother came and sat next to him. "It must have been hard seeing her after all these years."

Hard. Surprising. Exciting. And a few other things I can't really explain.

"I hope you two had a chance to talk."

"We did. She's divorced."

Her eyes lit up. *"Really?"*

Uh oh. That was the wrong thing to say, particularly since he hadn't decided anything one way or another. *I am too old for this.*

CHAPTER 4

"What do you mean you won't be back in time for the camping trip this weekend? I thought you were coming back today or tomorrow."

Byron shifted the cell to his other ear and straddled a lounger on the patio. "Something came up, so I'm staying for a couple of weeks." At least twice a year, Byron, his friend Sheldon Greer and two of his other Army buddies spent a weekend camping. However, they'd traded sleeping in tents on the hard, cold ground for a cabin with all the amenities, including cable TV.

"I hope it's not your parents," Sheldon said, his voice lined with concern.

"No, they're fine. I ran into an old friend this weekend and—"

He burst out laughing. "A woman, no doubt. And just how old a friend?"

Chuckling, Byron said, "Real old. High school old."

"Old girlfriend?"

"No." He gave his friend a rundown of what happened with Nzinga's parents.

"Man, that's some cold shit. She could've been your Mrs. Right. But I can understand where her parents were coming from, since I have two daughters. No way would I let some eighteen-year-old date my fifteen-year-old daughter. Sorry, bro."

"Yeah, you are sorry." In theory, it probably made sense, but his young heart couldn't understand it. All he saw was two people standing in the way of him and the girl he loved.

Sheldon laughed. "Well, I guess I can't be mad at you for wanting to spend some time with her. Is she retired, too?"

"No. She's a doctor."

"Even better. If you get sick, you can get a very personal physical."

"Nah, man. Nzinga's a pediatrician."

"Nzinga. Her name is different."

"It's the name of a 17th century Angolan queen who fought the Portuguese for the freedom of her people." Byron had been fascinated with her name and, after finding out the information had taken to referring to Nzinga as a queen.

"Ah, okay. Did you just find that out now or before?"

"The latter."

"Well, I can't be mad at you. If it was me, I'd do the same thing. There's nothing like coming home to my wife. It took me a long time to find her and she's made all the difference in my life." It had taken Sheldon until age forty-five to find his perfect woman, a divorcee with two teenage daughters. They would be celebrating their tenth anniversary later that year.

"I have no idea if anything will come of it, but it's been nice spending a little time with her. I'll catch you guys on the next trip."

"I'll let the guys know and we'll be expecting an update. It's the least you can do after backing out at the last minute."

Byron snorted. "Like you didn't do the same two years ago when Adele wanted to go to that jazz festival."

"You weren't supposed to remember that," Sheldon said with a chuckle.

"I'm not that old. I'll let you know when I get back. Later." He disconnected and shook his head. Their thirty-year friendship had withstood Desert Storm, Afghanistan and a host of other deployments. They were blessed to make it out alive and whole.

He placed the phone on the table next to him. The indoor patio gave him a good view of the setting sun, while avoiding the Sacramento heat. After a few minutes, he picked the phone up again, scrolled through the contacts to Nzinga's name and hit the call button. It was just after eight and he had waited to call to give her time to get home and relax first. At the same time, he didn't want to wait too late.

"Well, hello, Byron," Nzinga said when she answered.

Just the sound of her voice stirred something inside him. "How are you?"

She laughed. "Tired, but good. Everybody can't just up and retire."

"Hey, I didn't just *up* and retire. I worked my butt off for over three decades. I think I deserve a little free time. How much longer do you plan to work?"

"I hadn't really thought about it. I love the kids, watched them grow up and now some of them bring their babies to me. It's a great feeling to know they trust you with their most precious gifts."

Byron could hear the passion and dedication as she spoke and it left no doubt in his mind that she was a phenomenal health care provider. "Your patients are very fortunate to have you."

"I hope so. Did you get a chance to visit your parents?"

"Yesterday. My mom remembered you and called you smart and lovely."

"Aw, I thought your mom was so nice. Whenever Wes and I had to study or work on a project, she'd always make these fabulous snacks and say, 'you can't study without brain food.' Your dad never said much."

"If I tell her what you said, she'll want to see you in person. And my dad still doesn't say much. He says Mom talks enough for the both of them."

"Funny, my dad says the same thing about my mother."

They swapped childhood stories about their parents and the next Byron knew the sun had gone down, stars studded the black sky and the moon shone brightly. He'd called to ask about dinner and had yet to broach the subject because he had been enjoying their conversation. "I originally called to see which night this week would be better for dinner."

There was a pause on the line, then Nzinga said, "Thursday. My schedule isn't too heavy and I should be able to get out of the office by five."

"If the weekend is better, I can wait." Not exactly the truth. If he could, he would have figured out a way to visit tonight.

"No, Thursday is fine. What will you be doing with all your leisure time while the rest of us are working?"

"Wes and I are going to see the A's tomorrow night. We'll most likely leave midday and stop by Everett & Jones for an early dinner first.

"Oh, no you didn't say Everett & Jones. I haven't been there in so long."

She'd just given his opening for a future date. "Then we'll have to go sometime. But not for our first date."

"No?" Nzinga asked humorously.

"Absolutely not. First dates always require a nice restaurant with candles and soft music.

"I had no idea there were rules about first dates."

"Maybe you've been hanging out with the wrong men."

"Maybe so. Then I'm counting on you to show me how it's done."

Byron pulled the phone away from his ear for a brief moment and stared at the display. Obviously, the sweet, almost shy girl he'd known had changed and it stimulated him in more ways than one. "I'll do my best."

"As much as I enjoy talking to you, Mr. Walker, I need to go to bed. It's almost midnight and I have an early day."

"My apologies. I was enjoying myself so much, the time got away from me."

"No apologies needed. I'm looking forward to dinner."

"So am I. Sweet dreams."

"You, too."

Byron ended the call and smiled. Thursday couldn't get here soon enough.

"I can't believe you've been holding out on us," Val fussed. "You haven't given us any details on your date with Byron."

Nzinga shook her head. "What details are you looking for? You all were at the same place, so you saw everything."

"Not *everything*," Max said. "I didn't follow you home, so I have no idea what happened—kisses, touches, a hot night of sex."

"Max! Really? I'm not having sex with a man on a first date. A second one, either, for that matter. I barely even know him." Even as she said the words, something inside her said she did know Byron. She felt as if time hadn't passed and they'd picked up exactly where they left off. Yes, with his hard, toned body pressed against her and his lips on hers, he made her feel a desire she had forgotten about.

As if reading Nzinga's mind, Val snorted and said, "Girl, please. The way you two were laughing and talking seemed like you guys haven't missed a beat."

"Sis, I know Melvin was an ass and I don't know what you ever saw in him, but—"

"Dang, Max," Val cut in. "You don't have to go there."

"What? Nzinga knows how I felt about him. No need to start pretending otherwise now."

Nzinga couldn't do anything but laugh. From the moment she had introduced them to Melvin, Max always held the belief that he was a snake and "a little too oily" for her tastes. In hindsight, her friend had been right. At the time, Nzinga had been impressed by his crisp speech, handsome face and the fact that he had a job and goals.

"As I was saying, being with that idiot might make any woman want to ignore the entire male population—the fool I married had me thinking the same thing at one point—but, at least, give Byron a chance. If a man stared at me the way he was doing while y'all were slow dancing, I might've had to drag him off the floor right then."

Val screamed with laughter. "I know that's right. Did you see Darlene's face? I wanted to cheer. Ask Donna. Girlfriend was too mad. She was tossing back drinks left and right."

"I can't believe you two." As teens they spent hours giggling about one thing or another and nothing had changed. "Is Donna working late tonight?"

"Yep. She has some big case and had to meet with the client, who wanted to meet after hours. But getting back to you and Byron, when's the next date?"

"Tonight, which is why I need to get off the phone." She glanced over at the nightstand clock. "He'll be here at seven and that only leaves me an hour to get ready."

"Where are you going?" Max asked.

"Out to dinner. I assume it's going to be a nice restaurant

because he mentioned something about our first date needing to be somewhere with candles and soft music."

This time both Val and Max screamed and Max said, "If you make us wait five days for details again, I am so going to hurt you. And you never did say whether he kissed you or not."

Sighing, she said, "Yes, Max, he kissed me goodnight. A nice, sweet one."

"Mmm hmm, we should just go ahead and make plans for lunch on Saturday."

"Fine. You guys can come over here. I'll text you with a time tomorrow."

"You kids have fun," Val said.

"Bye." Nzinga placed her phone on the charger and went to change. For tonight's dinner, she'd chosen a simple sleeveless black and white sheath dress. She would take her wrap in case she needed it in the restaurant. As she dressed, her mind went back to her nightly phone calls with Byron. He was funny, engaging and flirted as well as he breathed. After that first night, she'd had to cut their conversations short because when she went to work on Tuesday, she could barely keep her eyes open. Back in the day, she could pull all-nighters, grab three or four hours of sleep and be fine. But that was then. Now, 1 a.m. bedtimes did not work well with having to get up at six-thirty in the morning. Tonight, she'd chosen to leave her hair up because it was too hot.

While waiting for Byron to arrive, she spent a few minutes going through the mail. There were at least three pieces that included invitations to medical conferences. She put them to the side, then tore the junk mail in half and dumped it in the trash.

Just like on Saturday, he handed her a single red rose when he arrived. "Hey, beautiful."

"Hi, yourself. Come on in."

Byron bent to kiss her cheek. "I forgot how hot it gets up here and it's not even the middle of summer yet."

Nzinga placed the rose in a small vase with the other one that was still hanging on, picked up her wrap and purse and walked back to where he stood. "Doesn't it warm up in LA?"

"Yes, but the temperatures start to cool off in the evening."

"No such luck here," she said, smiling. And that didn't help with the occasional hot flashes that had started a year ago. The only good thing was that they didn't occur frequently.

Once they were settled in the car, he cranked the air up. "You mentioned liking Italian food. Is Il Fornaio okay? I googled and found one not too far in the Roseville Galleria."

"That's fine, and it's only about fifteen minutes away." She couldn't believe he had been paying that much attention during their conversation about favorite foods. On the way, they conversed about everything and nothing. "You should just park in the garage. It's a little closer."

Following her directions, Byron entered the garage and found a spot near the front. "It's not too crowded tonight."

"Probably because it's a Thursday. Weekends are a different story, and I don't even want to think about the holidays. Once, it took me forty minutes to find parking. If I hadn't been with my mother, I would've gone home and shopped online."

His booming laughter filled the car's interior. "I thought women liked shopping."

"I like shopping okay, but not enough to be circling a parking lot forever to find a spot." He came around to her side and helped her out, but didn't let go of her hand. As if it were something he did all the time, he entwined their fingers and headed toward the restaurant. His strong, large hand engulfed her small one, but strangely, seemed to be a perfect fit. Inside, he gave his name to the hostess and they were led to a table with a window view. Almost immediately, a server came over to take their drink orders and left a plate with bread and olive oil and balsamic vinegar for dipping. Both opted for white wine.

Byron picked up his menu. "I've never been here before. Any recommendations?"

Perusing her own menu, Nzinga said, "Depends on what you like. I love the pasta dishes or the lasagna."

"I haven't had lasagna in ages," he murmured. "I think I'm going to have that."

She decided on the angel hair pasta with marinara sauce, tomatoes and basil. Not able to resist, she broke off a piece of bread, dipped it into the olive oil and popped it into her mouth. Bread was her weakness, but she planned to limit herself.

Once their drinks came and their orders given, he waited until the server left and lifted his glass. "To getting to know each other again."

Nzinga momentarily froze. Did he want to continue talking once he returned home next week? She lifted her glass and touched it to the side of his, then took a small sip. She guessed it was something they should talk about soon.

Byron reached across the table and took her hand. "Nzinga, seeing you again has been the best part of this visit." He angled his head thoughtfully. "I'm trying to see what's different about you and what's the same."

She laughed softly. "I should hope I've changed in almost forty years."

"Yes, but in all the ways it matters, you're exactly the same. Your smile, your laugh, the way your eyes light up when you're talking about your passions. The biggest thing I see that's the same is your heart. You still have a beautiful heart."

She snatched her glass up and took a big gulp. The way this man was staring at her... Max's words came back: *If a man stared at me the way he was doing while y'all were slow dancing, I might've had to drag him off the floor right then.* He had the same look now and the refined woman she'd always been wanted to be usurped by a new inner woman who missed the touch of a man. Pushing the thoughts aside, she said, "You haven't changed, either. I always remembered you being such a gentleman and having a kind heart." And the finest thing walking. Most guys would have tried to get her to go against her parents' wishes, but not Byron. As heartbroken as they had been, he respected their judgement and kept his distance. Even when she and Wes were studying, he never said more than hello or asked about her wellbeing. Those were the longest four months of her life. She had started having Wesley over her house to study, instead, something her mother hadn't complained about one bit.

"I appreciate you saying that. My father is my role model and I've tried to be the man he taught me to be."

"Well, I'm sure he's very proud," she said far softer than she had intended.

The server returned with their food and they ate in silence for a few minutes. This dating thing was a relatively new experience for her. Before her ex, she'd only had two boyfriends. Both couldn't deal with her school schedule and the relationships had faded within a few months. She had dated loosely, but, again, the men didn't understand the hours she put in as a new doctor or were intimidated by her. Nzinga hadn't hesitated to drop them like a bad habit. Melvin had played the role for a several years, but his true colors eventually came to light. In hindsight, Nzinga should have cut her losses far sooner. She had gone out with a guy a couple of months ago, but his only interest was in her bank account. Now there was Byron, who seemed to be everything she wanted in a man. Deciding to shift her mind to a less dangerous subject, she asked him about the trip to Oakland.

"We had a ball. The A's won, so that made it better. Oh, and the food at Everett & Jones..." Byron grinned.

Nzinga eyed him. "Don't start."

He laughed and shrugged. "I'm just saying. You asked me about the trip."

She rolled her eyes. "Whatever." But she was smiling. They continued to laugh and talk and linger over dessert.

Finally, he said, "I should probably get you home. We're going to have to make our next date on the weekend, so I can spend more time with you."

"We're going out again?"

"Absolutely. I've got to get it in before I leave next week."

Both fell silent with the implication. Once again, she wondered what would happen after he went home. Rather than speculate on it, she decided to enjoy it while it lasted.

When they got back to her house, Byron stopped just inside the door and pulled her into the circle of his arms. "I'm not going to stay because you need to be well rested for all those screaming babies."

Nzinga smiled. "I do have a full schedule tomorrow...with *lots* of screaming babies."

He tilted her chin. "Thank you for dinner."

He lowered his head and kissed her, softly at first, then more deeply. In the blink of an eye, it changed again, sending bolts of desire through her body. She moved closer to his body and her hands roamed up his arms and chest, ending around his neck Obviously, he had kept up with his workout regimen. For a man a few years off of sixty, she didn't feel one ounce of flab. At length, he lifted his head.

"Good night, my queen," he whispered. Byron stepped back out into the night and closed the door.

Nzinga slumped against it and closed her eyes. She hadn't

heard that name since the day she graduated. He'd looked it up and found that there had been an Angolan queen by the same name. He had told her she would always be a queen in his eyes, given her a gold necklace with a heart charm and kissed her. That kiss had been one of a teenager, but tonight's was that of an experienced man and her body still pulsed. That hot night of sex sounded *really* good at the moment.

CHAPTER 5

*S*aturday morning, Byron and Wesley stood in the backyard shooting hoops. It was only ten, but the temperatures had climbed to seventy-eight degrees already and it promised to be another hot day.

"This thing with Nzinga seems to be moving fast." Wesley tossed Byron the ball.

He took a shot and sank it. "Faster than I had planned." He lined up another shot and missed.

Wesley hit his next one. "What exactly are your plans?"

He had been asking himself the same question since dropping Nzinga at her door on Thursday evening. He had only called her his queen once after explaining why, but the endearment had slipped out on its own volition. "I want to continue getting to know her, to find out whether this is something or just some fantasy left over from high school."

"Could be complicated with you two living on opposite ends of the state."

"You don't think I know that," he said with an exasperated sigh, tossing the ball hard to his brother.

"Whoa. No need to bite my head off. I'm just bringing up the obvious."

Byron ran a hand over his head. "I know," he muttered. "This thing has got me so confused, I don't know whether I'm coming or going." A difficult admission for a man who prided himself on his ability to be in control at all times.

Wesley gave a short bark of laughter. "Welcome to the club. Loren had me feeling the same way. I couldn't eat or sleep and I wanted to call her the moment I woke up every day." He bounced the ball twice and hit a bank shot. "I remember this one time in college when I was sitting with my buddies and she walked past and smiled at me. Man, I lost my train of thought, dropped my sandwich and was grinning like an idiot. They never let me live that down."

The image brought on by that had Byron doubled over in laughter.

"Laugh all you want, but I got my girl."

"Yeah, you did." He and Loren had celebrated twenty-eight years of marriage in February. A pang of sadness hit Byron. He didn't begrudge his brother's happiness, though. Wesley and Loren still behaved like they were teenagers sometimes—stealing kisses, giggling over some whispered promise—much to their children's horror. Thinking back, Byron didn't have the same kind of relationship with either of the women he'd come close to marrying. He'd loved them, but he couldn't be as playful with them as he was with Nzinga. She had no problems bantering with him. The ball hit him in his chest, breaking into his musings.

"You playing or daydreaming?" Wesley asked with an amused smile. "For someone who's supposed to be a basket-ball star, your concentration ain't that great."

"Shut up. I can still wipe the floor with you without breaking a sweat." They continued the trash talk until the game ended with Byron winning by one point. "Guess my title holds."

"You were just lucky, old man."

"You're only three years behind me, so that makes you almost as old."

"But you'll always be older. Okay, I think I need a shower. My knees are going to be killing me tomorrow."

"Again...*old*. My knees are just fine. You'd better start getting out of the classroom and heading to the gym." Exercise had been so engrained into Byron's life, he had a hard time when he skipped more than two days. He still ran two miles at least three times a week and had a home gym set up in one of his two spare bedrooms.

"Yeah, yeah, I know. Loren says the same thing. She even offered to work out with me."

"If you're dropping food and grinning when she walks by, that might not work out too well. All you need is to drop a barbell on your chest. Not a good look."

Wesley muttered an expletive telling Byron just what he thought of his comment and stalked toward the patio door.

Byron roared with laughter and followed. Half an hour later and freshly showered, he made his way to the kitchen to season the ribs they would be having for dinner. With it being his last weekend in town, his mother wanted to have a family dinner. He loved his family, but he'd wanted to spend tonight with Nzinga talking, laughing and definitely kissing her. It had been difficult to walk away from her that night after their date. The way she touched, held and kissed him back had him aroused at a level he hadn't been in years.

He cut open the packages and trimmed the meat, then added his blend of seasonings and spices and placed them in Ziploc bags.

"Hey, Byron. That meat smells good," Loren said, coming into the kitchen.

"And it'll taste even better. You making your potato salad?"

"Yep. Mom has officially passed me the torch. Said she was getting too old to remember all the ingredients."

"My mother has the memory of an elephant," he said with a laugh. "That's her way of getting out of cooking and having us do all the work." His mother had created an elaborate menu with ribs, chicken, salmon, shrimp, the potato salad and about five other side dishes. But, somehow, she had shifted the bulk of the cooking to them, leaving her to make only a green salad and her pound cake.

"I know. She did the same thing at Thanksgiving and Christmas." She set the potatoes on the stove to boil, then pulled out several ears of corn.

Byron joined Loren at the bar and helped remove the husks.

"I really liked Nzinga and her friends. They remind me of my girlfriends. And I think you like her, too."

"I do."

"Nooo, I mean really like her, as in girlfriend or relationship like her." When he didn't respond, she said, "So, am I right?"

"Maybe."

"Please, with the way your face lights up when you're going to see her or when you're talking to her on the phone, you more than like her. And, you've been shopping three times for clothes in the past week. No man is going to willingly step foot into a mall once, let alone three times, unless he really likes a woman."

Byron conceded her that point. Because he hadn't planned on doing anything outside of relaxing, the only clothes he'd brought consisted of shorts and tees. In the week he had been there, he'd purchased a suit, dress shirt, two pairs of slacks and two silk polos.

"You're going to be putting lots of miles on your car and racking up a ton of frequent flyer miles, you know."

"Yeah." He'd thought about that as well. During his active military deployments, long-distance relationships were the norm, unless one happened to be dating another soldier. But he didn't think he could do that type of relationship now. He didn't *want* that type of relationship. It was just one more thing to think about. He and Loren finished the corn in companionable silence and, afterwards, he went to relax in his borrowed room. He picked up his phone and saw a text message from Sheldon: *I can't believe you left me here alone to deal with these two.* Byron clicked on the accompanying image of Bill and John posing with a beer in one hand and their biceps flexed on the other. He sent a reply: *Better you than me. Enjoying my time in Sac.*

An hour later, they packed up and made the drive over to his parent's house.

As soon as the family sat down to dinner, his mother asked, "Byron, have you talked to Nzinga since the reunion?"

He paused with his fork halfway to his mouth and met Wesley and Loren's amused expressions. Both tried to hide their smiles, but weren't doing a good job of it. "I talked to her a couple of days ago."

"Good. Then, there's hope for you yet."

Wes and Loren's laughter exploded and he shot them a glare. Even his niece and nephew were laughing, the traitors.

"Keep me posted, so I'll know if I need to find me a new dress."

Byron's mouth fell open. "Seriously, Mom? We're just friends." The lie even sounded hollow to him. He'd leaped past the friend zone the first time he kissed her. And none of his thoughts as of late could be considered remotely *friendly*. They all revolved around him and Nzinga naked and in his bed. As his brother said, things were moving fast. What scared Byron most was that he didn't care.

Nzinga carried a large bowl of salad greens and three bottles of dressing out to the sunroom and placed them on the table. When the judge awarded her the house as part of her divorce settlement, her first thought had been to put it on the market as soon as she walked out of the courthouse. However, she hadn't and was glad because she loved the area she had turned into her own comfortable space. One side of the room held a pair of loungers with a small bistro table between them, a fireplace and bookshelf. The other side held a buffet with a built-in wine rack and a dining table with seating for six. She went back for the tray holding bowls of chicken, shrimp and crab, and the bread basket. With the heat, she had opted for a lighter lunch. As soon as she started back to the kitchen, her doorbell rang. Nzinga changed directions and went to open the door and stepped aside. "Hey, Donna."

"Hey, Z." Donna held up an insulated bag. "I brought wine and it's already chilled. I figured we'd need some once we started talking about you and Byron." She followed Nzinga to the kitchen. "Seems like I missed out on some information."

"You didn't miss anything. The wine bucket is in the sunroom. How's it going with your new client?"

"Girl, this man wants us to investigate his entire company. He thinks everybody's embezzling. I've gotten home after eight three nights straight. The money he's paying is good, but I don't know if it'll be worth all the headache of him trying to tell me how to run my investigation."

"Hopefully, it won't turn out too bad. And the other parts of your life?" Nzinga took butter and plates out.

She smiled faintly. "I'm good."

"You'll let us know if you're not, right?" There had been a couple of times lately when Donna retreated into her shell. Either Nzinga, Val or Max would text Donna to make sure she was okay and let the other two know. They tried not to bombard her.

"Yeah, sis. I will."

She gave Donna's shoulders a reassuring squeeze. The doorbell rang again and she left Donna to go answer it. Both Max and Val were standing there.

"Hey, girl," Val said, entering. "I can't believe Donna beat us here."

After a round of hugs, they all went out to the sunroom and found Donna opening one of the wine bottles.

Max wandered over to the table and surveyed the spread. "I'm starving and this looks good. Since it's salad, I can indulge. These hips are taking on a life of their own, so I've been trying to exercise more and watch what I eat." At five eight, Max's size sixteen curves had been known to cause men to stumble.

"We can eat," Nzinga said. After everyone fixed their plates and sat at the table, the friends spent a few minutes catching up on each other's jobs. Donna repeated what she had told Nzinga.

Max laughed. "It would be crazy if it turned out the man was right." She forked up a bite of salad and chewed. "I'm thinking about reducing my hours. This body is getting too old to be moving down and up from the floor."

"How many hours?" Val asked.

"Maybe down to thirty or thirty-two—seven hours, Monday through Thursday and only four hours on Friday.

Caroline wants me to be a partner in the company, but I don't know if I want all that responsibility."

Nzinga nodded. "It's more than a notion. Some days I ask myself what I was thinking."

Max gestured with her fork. "My point exactly. If she'd asked ten years ago, I might have said yes, but now..." She shrugged.

"I like working for myself," Val said. "I can take cases when I want and turn down the ones I don't want. And since it's just Robin and I, the overhead isn't too bad." After a few minutes, Val changed the subject. "I've been meaning to tell you guys that Desmond had the nerve to send me a friend request on Facebook."

Donna rolled her eyes. "After the way he acted, he should've included an apology. Did you accept it?"

Val looked at her like she was crazy. "No. I hit that delete button so fast and hard, he probably felt it."

They fell out laughing. Once they calmed down, Max said, "That's almost as bad as Greg Hilton following me around after one dance, trying to get me to give him my phone number."

Nzinga wiped tears of mirth from her eyes. "Well, he's persistent, if nothing else. You know he's probably still mad that you wouldn't go with him to the homecoming dance junior year, junior prom and senior prom."

"What? Do I need to make him a sign that says, 'I don't like you' for him to get it?" She waved a hand.

Donna held up a hand. "I'm glad I didn't have those problems."

Max popped a piece of roll in her mouth. "If I threatened to break someone in half if they touched me, I wouldn't have them, either. The only one of us who seemed to hit the jackpot is Z. You were going to tell us about that date on Thursday," she added sweetly.

Three pairs of eyes focused on Nzinga. "We just went to Il Fornaio. I happened to mention that I loved Italian food and he remembered. I don't think Melvin ever remembered one thing I liked." She took a sip of her wine and wasn't sure she wanted to share her feelings, but they'd been confiding in each other since forever. "Is it crazy that I like Byron? I mean before last week, the mere mention of dating turned my stomach."

"Girl, no. You keep forgetting you guys had history," Donna pointed out.

"Not really. Outside of him kissing me on graduation—which y'all interrupted—he never made an attempt to do anything other than speak."

"Our bad," Max said. "But the fact that you and Byron liked each other then, even if it was from a distance, the feelings were still there. Who knows? This could be a second chance, and you don't have to worry about your parents interfering."

"He's going home next week sometime and I have no idea how any of that will work. He hasn't said anything about us keeping in touch."

Val toasted Nzinga with her glass. "Did he kiss you again after the date?"

She nodded.

"Another sweet one, or the kind that snatches your breath and makes you weak?"

"The latter," she mumbled.

"Oh, he's going to bring it up. Mark my words."

Max smiled. "Bet he had you thinking about that hot night of sex."

Nzinga paused, then confessed, "Oh, my goodness, *yes!*" She leaned back against the chair and let out a satisfied sigh and they all hollered. Her phone rang and she got up and went to the sideboard where she'd left it. When she saw

Byron's name on the display, she hesitated answering because she knew they'd tease her from now until eternity.

"Don't just stand there and stare at it," Val said. "We know it's Byron by the look on your face."

"Hush." She turned her back and answered.

"Good afternoon, beautiful lady."

"Hey, Byron."

She heard muffled voices in the background. "Sounds like you're busy."

"My mom wanted to have a family barbeque before I left. How's your day going?"

"Donna, Val and Max are over and we're having lunch."

"I'm sorry. I didn't mean to interrupt."

"You're not interrupting."

"Hi, *Byron*," they said in singsong, then broke out in a fit of laughter.

Nzinga whirled around and glared at them.

Byron's laughter came through the line. "I see they haven't changed, either."

"Not one bit."

"Are you going to be busy tomorrow?"

"I promised my cousin I'd come over and talk to her daughter, who's interested in going to med school."

"Oh."

She smiled at the disappointment in his voice. "But I don't have any plans in the coming week and the office is closing on Friday at noon."

"Can we spend Friday together?"

"Yes."

"Is there anything special you'd like to do?"

"No. Let's just play it by ear."

"Sounds like a plan. Tell the crew I said hello and I'll call you tomorrow."

"Okay. Enjoy your family." They spoke a moment longer,

then ended the call. She placed her hands on her hips. "What is wrong with y'all? Acting like we're still in high school." She tried to keep a straight face, but failed. She reclaimed her chair. "I can't with you three. Wait until you meet a guy. I'm going to remind you of all this."

Max gestured. "Bring him on. In the meantime, we'll just live our love lives vicariously through you."

Smiling, Nzinga picked up her wine glass. Despite the teasing, she couldn't deny the excitement she felt at the prospect of seeing Byron. It was going to be a long week.

CHAPTER 6

*A*s soon as Nzinga opened the door to him Friday afternoon, Byron pulled her into his arms and slanted his mouth over hers in a deep, passionate kiss. He'd waited all week to feel her body against his. When she ran her hands over his chest, he groaned. Feeling himself teetering on the brink of losing control, he eased back and rested his forehead against hers, both their breathing ragged. He closed his eyes briefly and tried to force air back into his lungs. At length, he lifted his head. "Hi."

"Hi. That was some greeting."

He merely smiled, not trusting himself to speak. With the rampant emotions stirring in his chest, he didn't want to scare her. Or himself.

"Did you decide on something to do?"

"Yep. I thought we'd head up to Oakland and—"

"Yes." Nzinga did a little dance. "Everett & Jones?"

He nodded. The way her eyes lit up had him wanting to give her anything she wanted. "I also saw that Euge Groove is playing at Yoshi's tonight and got us tickets for the seven-thirty show." He peeked at his watch. "It's almost two, but I'm hoping we don't run into too much traffic. Even if we do, we'll still have plenty of time for an early dinner before the show."

"I love jazz." She glanced down at herself. She had on a pair of black slacks, a gold printed blouse and flat sandals. "Is this okay?"

"Perfect." Byron had worn a pair of gray slacks and a black pullover silk tee. He figured going business casual would fit the bill at both places.

"I just need to get my jacket and I'll be ready. The temperatures near the water tend to cool off at night." She hurried off and came back in a flash.

They spent the two-plus hour drive—of course they ran into traffic—discussing their favorite music groups from then and now, and he found they had similar tastes. He thought about their previous conversations. From cuddling up eating popcorn and watching movies to enjoying NCAA and NBA games, she seemed to fit him better than any other woman.

Rather than search for parking on the street, he drove to the lot next to the jazz club. The restaurant was only a block away, so he wouldn't have to worry about moving the car later. "Would you like to take a walk first?"

"Sure. We picked a good day to come. The weather is really nice."

"And at least fifteen degrees cooler than in Sac." The eighty-degree weather in the Bay felt like spring time in contrast to the near one hundred degrees they'd left behind. There were two days left in June and July promised to be even more of a scorcher. Linking their hands together, they crossed the street, being careful of the railroad tracks and started a leisurely stroll near the water. It didn't take long for the block to get crowded.

"With all these folks dressed up, I bet they're going to the concert, too."

"We should probably get back a little early. If memory serves me correctly, you have to line up for seating and I want us to get good ones."

"Then we should go on over to have dinner now. I don't want to be stuck in a corner."

"Amen. These long legs don't do well in cramped spaces." Laughing, they changed directions and walked the block and a half over to the restaurant. They ended up having to wait about ten minutes for a table, which wasn't bad.

Nzinga stared at her menu. "I'm having a hard time choosing what to get."

"Then how about we share the four-way combination plate? That way you'll get ribs, chicken, brisket and the hot links. We can just get a couple additional sides."

"Works for me. Now for the sides," she murmured. By the time the server came over to take their order, she had decided on the greens and mac and cheese, and iced tea. When the young woman left, Nzinga said, "You have to drink tea with soul food."

"I wholeheartedly agree." Byron had consumed two glasses the last time he'd come. He'd gotten off his workout regimen and was going to have to ramp it up to offset all the calories he had consumed over the past two weeks. It didn't take long for their food to arrive with extra plates. He recited a short blessing and gestured for her to go first. He was in the middle of adding the brisket to his plate when he looked up and saw Nzinga lick barbeque sauce from her lips and fingers. Arousal hit him hard and fast and he had to turn away or risk jail for public displays of affection. *Have mercy!* "Good?"

"Yes. So good. Thanks for bringing me. You always seem to know the things I like."

Her stunned expression let him know she hadn't meant to say the words. Not wanting to make her uncomfortable, he chose not to respond. Instead, he picked up her hand and placed a kiss on the back. She visibly relaxed and he knew he had made the right decision. After they finished eating, he asked, "Would you like dessert?"

Nzinga rubbed her hands together and gave him a brilliant smile. "I think that sweet potato pie is calling my name. We can share, so I don't eat too much."

And she was calling *his* name. Byron hadn't anticipated how the intimate act would impact him, especially the way she slowly drew the fork out of her mouth each time. He had never been so glad for a dinner to end. Just as he suspected, the line outside of Yoshi's had already started to form when they arrived and the show didn't start for another forty-five minutes. Fortunately, there were only three couples ahead of them.

"Good call on getting here early."

They passed the time making small talk with the couple in front of them. When the doors opened, they were fortunate to get seating on the third row with an aisle behind them, which allowed him a little more room to stretch out in the cramped area. The way the small tables had been set up forced the two couples to sit in front of each other.

Nzinga rotated in her chair. "You okay back there?"

Chuckling, he said, "I'm fine."

During the show, she clapped and danced in her seat. "I am loving his music. I need to get a CD after the show."

Watching her animated features made Byron smile. He turned his attention back to the music and bobbed his head in time with the beat.

"That was fantastic!" she said when it ended and they filed out with the other patrons. It took a few minutes to get her autographed CD and she waved it in the air when she approached. "I got my CD and a picture. Can we sit on one of the benches near the water for a few minutes?"

"Of course." Byron wasn't ready for the night to end, so he had no problem granting her request. They headed back across the street and snagged an empty bench. He took a seat next to her and draped an arm around her shoulder. She leaned into him. They sat quietly for several minutes. "I'm leaving in the morning."

Nzinga lifted her head.

"These past two weeks with you have been nothing short of amazing, and I'm hoping we can continue to see each other."

"How are we going to do this?"

"The same way we're doing it now. It's nothing for me to make the drive, or fly up on a weekend, and I'd like to invite you to my house. I'll pay for your flight and I have a guest bedroom you can use."

She faced the water and didn't say anything for a minute, as if thinking over his proposal. Finally, she met his gaze. "Okay."

Byron released the breath he didn't realize he had been holding. "We can take things as slowly as you need, Nzinga, and I won't pressure you in any kind of way. I just want to have you in my life again."

"Byron," she whispered.

He touched his lips to hers. For the first time in a long while, his love life felt *right*.

Friday, Nzinga sat in her office charting, but her mind kept straying to Byron. It had only been a week since she'd seen him, but she missed him. Missed his smile, his laughter and, especially his kisses. She recalled everything about the past two weeks and tried to remember the last time she'd had so much fun with a man. He always seemed to do things that were special to her. When she'd blurted it out to him in Oakland, she had wanted to slide under the table. Byron hadn't said anything, as if he had known how uncomfortable she had been. Nzinga found it harder and harder to hide her growing feelings. Her mind said she was far past the age of falling for a man on sight, but the other parts of her didn't care. She reminded herself that, although the two of them had never officially dated, the strong emotional pull she'd felt all those years ago was still there. She wanted to attribute these new sentiments to some long-buried first crush, but the more time she spent with him, the more she was convinced it was something else. Something stronger. Something she had no control over.

Her gaze went to her cell sitting on the desk. They hadn't talked for the past two nights and she'd wanted to call him, but talked herself out of it each time. Before Nzinga lost her nerve again, she picked up the phone.

"Well, good afternoon, beautiful."

The deep, warm sound of his voice was enough to make her swoon in the chair. "Good afternoon, handsome," she said, surprising herself. "How's your day going?"

"Not bad. Went for a run, worked out in my home gym and just got out of the shower."

Nzinga tried her best not to think about him naked in the shower, rivulets of water running down his hard body. She closed her eyes to shut out the images, but they kept coming, along with a soft pulsing between her thighs.

"Nzinga."

Her eyes snapped open. "What? I'm sorry, what did you say?"

"Are you okay?"

"Oh, yes. Fine."

"I asked if you were still at work."

"I am. I have two more patients before I can call it a day. What about you?"

"I'm meeting a few of my Army buddies for drinks." Byron paused. "Are you going to be busy next weekend?"

She mentally ran down her calendar. "I don't think so. Why?"

"I'd like to invite you down."

Her heart started pounding. If she went, it would be a turning point. Nzinga asked herself if she was ready. Her grandmother's words rang in her ears: *Tomorrow is not promised, so don't waste time when you could be happy.* "I'll be there."

"Thank you," he said quietly. "I know this seems crazy, but—"

"I understand and I'm feeling the same way."

He laughed. "Thank goodness. I thought I was out here by myself."

"No, you're not."

"Dr. Carlyle, your next patient is here. Room two."

Nzinga turned toward the medical assistant and said, "I'll be right there." Turning her attention back to the call, she said, "My next patient is here."

"I'll make the flight arrangements and text the itinerary to you, if that's okay."

"It's okay. Talk to you soon." She disconnected and smiled. She couldn't wait to tell her girls.

Nzinga grabbed her iPad and headed down the hallway to the examination room. "Hi, Mrs. Jackson. How's Aiden?"

The woman laughed. "A lot better than I am. Obviously, those antibiotics worked because he's back to driving me crazy."

She smiled down at the toddler, who was dancing around the room, a stark contrast to the crying little boy grabbing at his ears on the last visit. She'd treated him for an ear infection. "Hi, Aiden. How are your ears?"

He grinned and raised his hands for Nzinga to pick him up. She set the iPad on the counter and lifted Aiden into her arms. It was days like this that brought home the emptiness of not being able to experience motherhood. Nzinga tickled him and he burst out in a fit of giggles. "Okay, big boy, let's look in your ears." She placed him on the exam table and Mrs. Jackson stood to hold Aiden still. She checked both his ears and was pleased to find all traces of the infection gone. "All clear. I think this deserves a prize." Nzinga had bought small toys for the children to choose from whenever they came for a visit.

"And that's why all my kids get excited to come to the doctor." Mrs. Jackson shook her head. "You can't retire for the next fifteen years until Aiden graduates from high school."

She laughed. "I'll see what I can do." That would put her at close to seventy and she didn't know if she'd still have the temperament or ability to deal with children at that age. After getting the toy and seeing them out, she made her way to the next room.

The first thing Nzinga did when she got home two hours later was strip out of the slacks and blouse and change into shorts and a tank, and turn up the air conditioner. She checked the time—five-thirty. She'd give Donna a little more time to get home before getting them all on the line. Then she did something that had been on her mind since reconnecting with Byron.

"Hi, Mom."

"Nzinga, baby. How are you?"

"I'm good. How are you and Dad doing?" They'd moved back to their hometown of Little Rock, Arkansas twenty years ago to take care of her father's mother and ended up staying.

"Doing okay. Old Arthur is giving us both fits, but that's nothing new."

She laughed. "What's the doctor saying?"

"Not much he can do, so don't you go worrying. We're alright. Is your life getting back together after that mess with Melvin?"

"It's fine." Her father had been ready to fly down and do bodily harm to Melvin, especially after Nzinga told them about the investment account and the child.

"Good. How was the reunion?"

"We had a lot of fun. They resurrected the jazz band and Valina pulled out her drumsticks and played. It was good to see some of the people. Actually, Byron happened to be in town visiting Wesley and came to the picnic."

"Byron Walker? The older boy who was sweet on you?"

"Yes." All the pain and hurt rose in her chest again.

She heard her mother's long sigh. "Baby, I know you were upset and hurt by our decision, but we were only doing what we felt was best. Maybe his intentions were honorable, but Byron was eighteen and on his way to college. The law considered him an adult and I didn't want him or you to get into any trouble."

"I know, and I was mad for a long time." Her mother had never quite put it that way. "I'm okay now. We've actually been talking. He recently retired from the Army."

"Talking how—as friends or something else?"

"I think something else."

She laughed. "You *think*? Honey, you'd better be sure. You're not that young girl anymore and have a good head on your shoulders. We're so proud of the woman you've become, and there's nothing standing between you two now. Just be careful."

A smile curved her lips. Leave it to her mom. Margaret Carlyle always had a way with words. "I will." Nzinga nixed the idea of mentioning to her mother about Byron flying her down for a visit. Some things a girl just didn't tell her mother, no matter her age. It brought to mind the sleeping arrangements once she arrived. He'd mentioned having a guest bedroom, but did she really want to stay in that room? Her mother's voice drew her out of her thoughts.

"Have you told your brother yet?"

"No. I haven't talked to him since last month." Two years her senior, Isaac, Jr. worked for a multi-national engineering firm in Atlanta and traveled a good portion of the time. They tried to catch up at least once a month.

"Keep me posted."

"Okay."

"For what it's worth, Nzinga, I always thought Byron was a nice and respectful young man. If he's the one for you, you'll know."

"That means a lot, Mom," Nzinga said around a lump in her throat. She swiped at a tear rolling down her cheek. "I love you."

"I love you more, sweetheart."

"I'll talk to you soon. Tell Dad I love him, too."

"Will do. Talk to you later."

She ended the call and held the phone against her heart. After composing herself, she called Max. A minute later, all four of them were on the conference call.

"I know you're calling to give us the latest update," Max said.

Rather than beat around the bush, she chose to just say it. "Byron is flying me down to LA next weekend." There was silence for a full minute before her three friends erupted in excitement.

"Sis, are you sure this is what you want to do? It seems kind of fast," Donna, always the logical one, said.

Val chuckled. "Donna, we're in our fifties, not twenties. I say go for it."

"What are you doing tomorrow? We have to go shopping for some good stuff. Hold on. Let me pull my calendar up."

Leave it to Max, with her outrageous self. Nzinga couldn't wait for her friend to find a nice man and wondered if she would be just as fired up. "I don't need anything new."

"You need sexy lingerie, girl."

"He has a guest bedroom that he mentioned."

"I bet you twenty dollars you don't sleep in that guest room one night," Max said emphatically.

"Yeah, sorry, Nzinga. I'm going to have to side with Max on this one."

"Donna, I can't believe you. You're always my voice of reason."

"I know, but after listening to you talk, I think this is a good thing."

"So, does that mean we're on for shopping tomorrow?"

"Max, I can't with you, girl," Val said. "But I'm in."

Nzinga laughed. "Fine. We go shopping." They chose a time and hung up. She sat there a moment longer, then got up and went to her closet. In a back corner, she retrieved a container that held her high school mementos. Taking it back to the bed, she sat on the edge and searched for an item. Nzinga located it near the bottom and with shaking hands picked up the small gray velvet box and opened it. Inside, lay the gold necklace with a heart charm that Byron had given her as a graduation gift. Because she hadn't wanted her parents to know, she had never worn it. But she would now to let him know she was ready for wherever this journey took them.

CHAPTER 7

"*H*ey, big brother. Do you have a minute?"

Byron paused in putting on his shoes and picked up the phone from the nightstand. He deactivated the speaker. "What's wrong?" Wes never started a conversation with that question unless he had something on his mind.

"Nothing."

He blew out a long breath. "Man, don't scare me like that. The last time you called and asked me that question was when Mom had to go to the hospital."

Wesley laughed softly. "Sorry."

"What's on your mind?"

"I was calling to see how things were going with Nzinga. Are you two still talking?"

"Yes. Why?"

"I know you've been through a lot with regards to women and I guess I just don't want to see you get hurt again if things don't work out."

"I'm a big boy, Wes, and I think I can handle whatever happens. I'm way past the age of playing games, not that I ever did, and I wouldn't pursue this if I didn't think it could lead to something special. You, of all people, knew how I felt about her." Wes had been the only person with whom Byron had actually shared his pain, although his parents had figured it out without him having to utter one word.

"I did. I really want it to work out for you and Nzinga. She's always been a good friend."

"No one wants it to work out more than me. She's everything I could ask for in a woman." He smiled thinking about them laughing and talking late into the night about any and everything. "Anyway, I need to get going. I'm meeting Sheldon, Bill and John tonight."

"Enjoy, and I'm happy you have a second chance to get your girl."

"Me, too. Later." Yes, he had a second chance with Nzinga and he planned to make it count. Byron finished dressing and left for the bar and grill.

Sheldon and Bill were already there when he arrived.

"Well, if it isn't the defector."

"Shut the hell up, Bill." He slid into one of the two empty chairs at the table. He glared at Sheldon. "Exactly what did you tell him?"

Sheldon shrugged. "The truth. You met some pretty, young thing and kicked us to the curb."

"Keep talking and I *will* be doing some kicking." A server came to the table and he ordered a beer. "Where's John?"

"He should be here any minute," Bill said. "I talked to him an hour ago and he said he'd be here."

On the heels of his statement, Byron saw John weaving his way to their table.

"What's up, my brothers?" John asked, taking a seat.

The men spent several minutes catching Byron up on the weekend trip he had missed. There had been a mix up with their reservation and the three had to spend the first night in a cramped one-bedroom cabin, instead of the spacious four-bedroom they expected.

John gestured toward Sheldon. "By the time this one here finished with the manager, we ended up having the entire room comped."

"Hell, it was the least they could do," Sheldon said. "My back is still killing me from sleeping on that small sofa."

"I'm sure Kyra would be happy to help you out. Then again, I'm still trying to figure out what she sees in your old ass."

Byron and Bill roared with laughter, while Sheldon shot John a dark glare. The banter stopped long enough for the drinks to arrive and for their food orders to be taken.

"So, Byron, who's this new woman you dissed us for?" Bill asked.

Byron took a swig of his beer. "*Dissed?* So that's what you're calling it? Her name is Nzinga and she's not a new woman. I've known her since high school." He filled them in on what had happened all those years ago, including her friendship with his brother.

John shook his head. "Man, that's cold. Most guys would've tried to get with her on the downlow, regardless of what her parents said."

"True, but I respected her more than that." It killed him having to see her and keep his distance. "The thing is I just happened to be in Sac the weekend of Wes's high school reunion."

Sheldon toasted Byron with his beer bottle. "Man, that's a sign it was meant to be."

"Maybe. We'll see."

"Well, do you have any pictures of this mystery woman?"

He pulled out his cell, scrolled through the photos, brought up the one of him and Nzinga at the reunion dinner and handed the phone to Sheldon.

"I can see why she has your nose wide open. She's a beautiful woman." Sheldon passed the phone to Bill and John, who echoed the sentiments.

John said, "If it doesn't work out, I'll be happy to step in."

For the first time in his life, Byron felt what could only be described as jealousy. The thought of Nzinga with any other man had him ready to punch his friend, even though he knew it had been a joke. It made him realize that his feelings were far deeper than he had been willing to acknowledge. He still didn't know how she felt. He'd been afraid to ask. Something in his expression must have changed because when he looked up, they were all staring at him.

"You love her," John said simply.

"I...I don't know."

"Yeah, you do. It's a good thing looks don't kill because you all would be planning my funeral right now." He handed Byron the phone and clapped him on the shoulder. "It's okay. We've all been there. If my Regina was still here, I'd be doing the same thing." His wife had died five years ago of breast cancer.

They all fell silent, remembering how devastated John had been. Byron, Bill and Sheldon had stood by him and his two sons at the gravesite and made sure one or more of them had been available for the first several months for whatever John and his family needed. The bond they had formed in officer school had strengthened and grown over the years and there was nothing one wouldn't do for the other. The food arrived and, after a few moments, the mood lifted and they were back to laughing. Two hours later, they said their goodbyes and made plans for the next meetup.

When Byron got home, he went straight to his bedroom and searched for flights. Was he really falling in love after only a few short weeks? The answer came back a resounding *yes.* A weekend wouldn't be nearly enough time, but for now, he'd take it. *For now.*

A case of nerves hit Nzinga the moment the plane landed in LA. She had never done anything like this in her life. Even now, she still didn't know if she had made the right decision. As they taxied to the gate, she sent a quick group text to Val, Donna and Max to let them know she'd arrived, as promised. She retrieved her carryon, deplaned and headed downstairs. With his towering height, it didn't take her long to spot Byron. The smile he gave her made her heart skip and all the butterflies dissipate. *This was the right decision.* Before she made it to the bottom of the escalator, he was there, taking her bag and kissing her with an intensity that snatched her breath. "Oh, my."

Byron grinned sheepishly. "I usually don't get carried away like that, but woman, you make me lose myself."

"You don't hear me complaining."

They shared a smile. His gaze dropped to her chest, then back up to her face. "You still have it," he said, emotion clearly evident in his voice.

She fingered the necklace. "Yes."

Byron stroked a finger down her cheek. "Do you have any other bags?"

"Nope. Just this one."

"I've never seen a woman travel with so little luggage."

She playfully punched him in the arm. "I'm only going to be here for two days. I don't need twenty sets of clothes."

"If you say so." He grasped her hand as they walked out to where he'd parked his car in the lot. Once he got them underway, he asked, "How was the flight?"

"Short and on time," Nzinga said with a laugh. "My kind of flight. So what's on the itinerary this weekend?"

"A little relaxation and, maybe, some sightseeing." Byron slanted her a quick glance. "Anything special you want to do?"

"Not off hand. I haven't been here in so long, I don't even remember what it's like. What I do know is this traffic is ridiculous." They were still trying to make it out of the airport and it was bumper-to-bumper.

"They've been working on the airport for I don't know how long and it doesn't look like they'll be done any time soon. LA's traffic is pretty bad, but hopefully, at this hour, it won't take too long to get home."

Nzinga made herself comfortable and watched the passing scenery. At the pace they were driving, she had time to see just about everything. Finally, it cleared and he made the rest of the drive easily. When he pulled into his driveway, those darn butterflies came back in full force. After getting out of the car, he led her up the walk to the one-story home and unlocked the door.

"Welcome to my home." He stepped aside to let her enter first.

She was immediately struck by the open layout with its polished wood floors, elegant furnishings and cathedral ceilings. Each room flowed seamlessly into the other.

"This is lovely, Byron."

"Thanks. Come on. I'll show you to the guest room."

Nzinga followed him down a short hallway and he stopped at the second door and hit the light switch. The room had been decorated in soft grays and blues. She tried to keep her mind from going there, but wondered how many other women had slept there previously.

"I hope the bed and the colors are okay. I went with a

queen-sized mattress and remembered you had some of these colors in your sunroom."

Her gaze flew to his. "Are you telling me you bought all this for...?" She tried to wrap her mind around his words. In that moment, she fell a little harder.

"Is it alright?"

"It's more than alright. But you didn't need to go through all this trouble."

Byron rolled her bag just inside the door and slid his arm around her waist. "It was no trouble, baby."

Baby? Did he just call me baby? She needed a minute. "Can I freshen up a bit."

"Sure. I'll be in the kitchen." He kissed her softly. "I'm glad you're here." He backed out of the room and closed the door.

Nzinga crossed the floor and collapsed on the bed. Things were moving so fast, she could barely keep up. She sat a few minutes longer, then changed into a comfortable pair of crop pants and a T-shirt. Afterwards, she searched out Byron and found him standing at a counter slicing something. "What are you doing?"

"I thought we could watch a movie and I figured we could have some brain food to snack on."

"Brain food?" Curious, she walked over to where he stood and peered around his shoulder. He was cutting tortillas into triangles. A foot away sat a deep fryer.

"Yep. Your favorite study food was my mom's homemade salsa and chips."

She stared at him in wonder. "How did you know that? I never mentioned it to you. Did Wesley tell you?"

He paused and propped a hip against the counter. "No. I saw how your eyes lit up every time she made it for you guys and I heard you tell her she made the best salsa anywhere."

She didn't know what to say. Even though they had been forbidden to date, he still paid attention to all her likes and, nearly forty years later, still had them committed to memory. At that moment she fell completely in love with him. Again. "I can't believe you remembered."

"You'd be surprised by what I remember, like the way you used to bite on your bottom lip when you were concentrating, or tap the end of your pencil against your chin when you were thinking about something." He shifted his body closer. "Or when you bounced your knees when you were nervous. I remember everything about you, Nzinga Carlyle," he said in a heated rush.

Everything she felt for this man rose to the surface and she pulled him down into a kiss, trying to convey the words she couldn't say. He quickly took over and swirled his tongue around hers with a finesse that made her want to drag him to the nearest bed.

"We should probably slow down," Byron said, still trailing kisses along her jaw and over her throat.

"Why?" she whispered.

His head came up sharply. "What are you saying?"

Nzinga gave him a coy smile. "If I have to spell it out for you—" He didn't give her a chance to finish her sentence before he unplugged the fryer, grabbed her hand and nearly sprinted down the hall to his bedroom.

Byron ran his hands up and down her bare arms. "Are you sure about this?"

She placed a finger against his lips. "I'm sure."

"This is not a casual thing for me, Nzinga. I want all of you."

"I want you, too."

He searched her face, as if looking for any doubts. Satisfied, he lowered his head and kissed her again while slowly removing her clothes and backing her toward his huge bed. He laid her in the center and kissed his way from her mouth to her ankles, lingering here and there and making her feel like she was coming out of her skin. Moans spilled from her lips, as he set her whole body on fire. He moved upward and cupped her breasts in his hands, kneading and massaging them. He took one pebbled nipple into his mouth, then the other, while his hand charted a path down her front to the softness between her thighs. Nzinga sucked in a sharp breath. He slid one, then two fingers inside her, slowly moving them in and out. He increased the pace and her thighs began to tremble. "Byron." Without warning, an orgasm hit her and she cried out.

"I've waited so long for you." He lifted his head and locked his eyes on hers, both recognizing the significance of the moment.

Tears leaked from the corners of her eyes with his passionate confession and he wiped them away with the pad of his thumb. He kissed her once more, then stood to undress and don a condom. As she suspected, his slim, muscular body was in good shape. He had a body of a man at least twenty years younger. She sat up and ran her hand over his wide chest and flat abdomen.

The bed dipped as he climbed onto it and lowered his body on top of hers, being careful not to place all his weight on her. "I know it may sound strange, but on some level, I think you've always had my heart."

Nzinga shuddered as he parted her thighs and positioned his erection at her entrance. He pushed gently, slowly until he was buried deep. The play of passion on his face heightened her own desire. She understood it. She was there, too. Their blended moans filled the room as he set a leisurely pace with long deep strokes, while his hands continued to caress her hip, sides and breasts. No man had touched her this way, as if she were priceless, precious.

He leaned down and crushed his mouth to hers. His

thrusts came faster and his groans grew louder. "Nzinga," he said almost reverently. "My beautiful queen."

He certainly made her feel that way. Each stroke brought her closer and closer to the edge and, this time, the pressure started deep in her belly and flared out to every part of her body. She came again, spasms racking her body for what seemed like forever.

A moment later, Byron went rigid above her and he let out a low groan as his body shuddered, his breathing harsh and uneven. "You're mine."

With aftershocks still flowing through her, Nzinga had to agree. She *was* his.

CHAPTER 8

*N*zinga clapped a hand over her mouth to stifle her laughter. She almost choked on the bite of sandwich in her mouth. "I'm at the office, Byron. Stop making me laugh." It had been three weeks since her visit to LA and the incredible nights they had shared. He'd taken her to Universal Studios Hollywood and they finally got around to watching movies while cuddled in his oversized recliner and eating her favorite homemade chips and salsa. Byron had perfected his mother's recipe and it tasted as good as she remembered.

"What? I didn't do anything. I just asked if you recalled the woman on the studio lot tour nearly jumping out of the tram when that fake jaws shark came out the water."

"Exactly my point. You shouldn't be laughing at her." During the two-hour tour at Universal Studios, they'd passed the Bates Motel from Alfred Hitchcock's *Psycho*, the plane wreckage from *War of the Worlds*, a chase from *Fast & Furious* and several other stops. But when the tram stopped on the "broken" bridge and the shark came out of the water, a woman sitting nearest to the action leaped over three people and nearly fell out the other side. Had it not been for two men seated there, she would have, no doubt, ended up in the water. She and Byron had tried to keep a straight face, but failed miserably, along with every other person on the tour, and they had been laughing about it ever since.

"Hey, you were laughing, too."

"Whatever."

"Miss you, baby."

"I miss you, too," she said softly. It was the first part of August and they had been seeing each other for almost two months. Though they talked by phone, text and videoconference almost daily, she missed his presence. When'd she embarked on the relationship, it didn't dawn on her how hard it would be not seeing him regularly. She hesitated asking because she didn't want to come off as needy, but she really wanted to see him. "Are you planning to come up sometime soon?"

"I have to. Three weeks is a long time without you in my arms. I enjoy the phone calls and texts, but I need to touch and kiss you."

He'd echoed her thoughts. "And I love when you touch and kiss me."

"Then I'll be sure to touch and kiss you until you're breathless. Until you can't think of anything except what I'm doing to you. I'm going to—"

Her pulse skipped. "I think we need to end this call." It would *not* look good for her colleagues to pass by the office and hear her moaning from having phone sex. And at her age!

Byron's low rumble of laughter floated through the line. "We'll continue tonight then, my queen."

"Yes. *Tonight*, when I'm at home. I'll talk to you later." Nzinga disconnected, tossed the phone on her desk and leaned her head back against the chair. "This man is going to get me in trouble," she mumbled. With the way the last few calls had gone, she was going to have to ban him from calling her during her work hours. *Thank goodness it's Friday.* The last thing she needed was to be exhausted from sexual frustration while trying to deal with children and their parents. She finished the last few bites of her turkey sandwich and pretzels and discarded the wrappers. A knock sounded and she went to open the door.

"Dr. Carlyle, these just arrived for you." The medical assistant had a huge grin on her face as she handed Nzinga a crystal cut vase filled with a dozen red roses. "This new guy you're dating wouldn't happen to have any nephews, would he?"

Nzinga laughed as she took the vase and placed it on her desk. "Sorry, Dina. He has one nephew who's seventeen, far too young for you." The twenty-seven year-old often lamented about not being able to find a guy who wasn't trying to get into her panties or wanting her to foot the bill for most of their dates.

"Too bad. Keep me posted on any long-lost cousins," Dina said with a laugh as she started back down the hall.

She glanced over at the gorgeous flowers and smiled. *Yep, he's a keeper.* She floated through the rest of her day and, not even a mother who came in yelling about her son still not being able to keep food down after a week, messed with her mood. As it turned out, the woman had not followed Nzinga's dietary instructions—broths, clear liquids and a few soft foods. Instead, she had continued to feed the child whatever he wanted, citing him not liking the suggested options as a reason.

Nzinga's smile was still in place by the time she made it home. She placed the flowers on her bedroom dresser where she could see them in the mornings when she rose and at night when she went to sleep. After changing into something more comfortable, she went to call Byron. She wanted to thank him for the gift. However, it rang as soon as she picked it up. "Hey, Max. What's up?"

"That's what I'm calling to find out. How're things progressing with Mr. Fine and Sexy."

She laughed. "They're going great. He sent me roses at work today."

"Aw, that's so sweet."

"It was."

"Have you guys discussed how you're going to continue to make this work?"

"No." And it was one of the things weighing heavily on her. "It's only been a couple of months, but I love him and these sporadic visits are getting harder and harder."

"I can totally see that. Maybe you should ask the question and see what he's thinking."

"Max, I can't do that. He might think I'm trying to get him to make some type of commitment he's not ready to make. And then, who's going to be the one to move? I'm not planning to retire any time soon and I don't feel right asking him to move."

"I hear you, sis, but I truly don't believe Byron will see it that way. I know he loves you. He fell in love with you the moment he laid eyes on you at that picnic," Max said with a chuckle. "We all saw it and I half expected him to throw you over his shoulder and take off. Let me find a man who'll look at me like that...yes, honey!"

"I can't wait for the man who's going to make you eat those words. And he's coming. We'll see if you're still spouting all this stuff about your own love life."

"I wish. But I've given up on finding someone who even remotely loves me the way Byron does you."

Even though Max tried to disguise it, Nzinga still heard the trace of sadness in her friend's voice. "He's out there, and he's going to treat you far better than Rolando ever did."

"If you say so. We sure know how to pick them, don't we? The only one who ended up with a good man was Valina. If Brad hadn't died in that fire, they'd still be married."

"And acting like giggling teenagers," she added, laughing. Bradley Anderson had loved his wife to distraction, and when the firefighter died in a warehouse fire twelve years ago, Val had been devastated and they didn't think she'd make it.

"Exactly. Anyway, back to you. Promise me you'll talk to Byron. If anybody does, you two deserve to be happy."

"Maybe I'll bring it up this weekend. Speaking of the weekend, what are you going to be doing?"

"Teresa and I are going to lunch. She's been complaining about her big sister neglecting her." Teresa was a decade younger than Max and loved her older sister dearly.

"Tell her I said hi."

"I will. She saw the T-shirt Monique made us and wanted to know why she couldn't have one. I told her she wasn't *seasoned* enough."

Nzinga burst out laughing. "Yeah. Tell baby girl she still has some living to do."

"I'll talk to you later."

"Bye, girl." After ending the call, she sat for a moment thinking about Max's suggestion. Nzinga and Byron had been able to talk about everything big and small, including their failed relationships. A part of her wanted to believe he'd be open to a discussion about their future, but the part of her who enjoyed finding love again wasn't so sure she wanted to rock the boat. At any rate, they would have to talk about it, and sooner, rather than later.

∼

"Are you sure this is want you want to do, Byron?" Sheldon asked. "I mean this is a big step, and you two have only been dating a couple of months."

"A couple of weeks, a couple of months, a couple of years...the time makes no difference. I love Nzinga and I'll do whatever I need to do to have her in my life." Byron wished he could go back and recapture all the time they had lost, but he couldn't. They'd lost so many years and, as he had done many times over the past two months, he tried not to speculate what his life might have been like had things turned out differently. "I've already talked to a realtor about putting the Manhattan Beach house on the market and started looking for something in Sac."

"You're not wasting any time."

"No."

"Well, I guess we'll have to coordinate having these camping trips now."

"Lake Tahoe has some nice cabins. I stayed in one right on the lake." He wondered if Nzinga would like to take a trip with him.

"Maybe we can double date, do one of those cruises and a fancy dinner. I'd like to meet Nzinga."

"You read my mind. I'll let you know."

"Any plans for the weekend? Since you're about to be a defector, I figured we could get together and roast you one last time."

He chuckled. "It'll have to wait until next weekend. I'm just getting to Sac."

"Wait. You didn't say anything about going up this weekend."

"I didn't know. I just woke up and decided to drive up and ask Nzinga to marry me." There was silence so long, Byron thought the call had dropped. "Sheldon, you still there?"

"Ah, yeah. When you said you were moving back home, I

figured you two would continue dating for a few months, then get engaged."

"I don't need to date her for months to know I want her as my wife. I keep telling you, but you act like you don't believe me."

Sheldon let out a loud sigh. "I guess I do now. Can you at least come back so we can throw you a bachelor party?"

"As long as you tell Bill there will be no strippers."

"True that. I'd never been so uncomfortable in my life." For Sheldon's get-together, Bill had been in charge of entertainment, but none of them thought he would hire a stripper. Byron and Sheldon had ended up hiding in a corner of the rented space to get away from the action. "I think I'll be in charge of the entertainment this time."

"Thanks. Appreciate it. I gotta go and call Nzinga."

"If she's been as miserable as you've been without her, she's going to be happy to see you."

"I hope so, particularly since she doesn't know I'm coming." Byron hoped she had liked the roses.

He let out a short bark of laughter. "You are one of a kind, colonel."

"I hope so."

"Let me know the date, so I can dust off my tux."

"Will do." He turned onto the quiet street with its stately homes and manicured lawns and parked in front of Nzinga's house. He hit the call button.

"Are you calling to get me in more trouble?"

"I certainly hope so. Now, where did I leave off? Oh, yeah, it was somewhere around me touching and kissing you. I think I should make good on that promise."

"What are you talking about?"

Grinning, Byron hit the end call button and hopped out the SUV. He strode up to her door and rang the bell. The look on her face when she opened the door was priceless and he wished he'd captured it.

Nzinga gasped. "I can't believe you're here."

He lifted her in his arms, kicked the door shut and slanted his mouth over hers in a kiss that he hoped conveyed all the love and passion he felt for her. When he finally had enough for the moment, he eased her back to the floor. "How was that for a start?"

She made a show of thinking. "It'll do...for starters. What are you doing here?"

He withdrew the small velvet box, opened it, and lowered himself to one knee. "I came to ask you to be my wife. I love you, Nzinga and I always have. I want to spend the rest of my life showing you just how much you mean to me. We missed out on a lot of years," he continued as emotion gripped him, "and we can get those back. I don't want to miss out on any more. This is our time and, if you say yes, I'll never give you a reason to regret it."

"Oh, my goodness. *Yes!*"

Byron slid the ring onto her finger and rose to his full height. "Thank you for making me the happiest man alive. You are my heart." His finger touched the heart charm on the necklace he'd given her. That she'd taken to wearing it filled him with quiet pride.

"I am so happy," Nzinga squealed. "Wait. How are we going to do this? I mean, where are we going to live? I have my practice and—"

He placed a finger on her lips. "Relax, sweetheart. I've already put my house in LA on the market and I'm looking for one here. I know you have this house, but I'd like us to have one that's ours."

She lifted a brow. "When do you want to get married? I'll put it on the market today. As long as you're there and I can have my sunroom, it's all good."

He threw his head back and laughed. "Woman, you are priceless. As far as a date, how about next month?"

"That soon?"

"I really wanted to say next week, so..." He shrugged.

Nzinga shook her head. "You are so crazy."

"Maybe. But you love my crazy self."

"That I do. Okay, next month. We can do something small."

"I want to go all out. This will be my first and only wedding and I want it to be extra special."

"Well, since you put it that way. We've got a lot to do and we need to get started." She turned and walked away, talking about venues, flowers, food and a host of other things.

Byron caught her hand. "Later. Right now, I want to make love to my future wife." He swept her into his arms, strode to her bedroom and gently laid her on the bed. For a moment, he just stared at her, thankful that she'd come into his life again. He slid onto the bed next to her and began his touch and kiss quest. "I'm going to touch you and kiss you until you ask me to stop, starting right here." He placed fleeting kisses along her eyelids, jaw, lips and the exposed column of her neck. Pushing up her top, he continued between the valley of her breasts and her soft belly. Her passionate gasps and moans made him as hard as he'd ever been, and it took a concerted effort not to just strip them both naked now and bury himself deep inside her. They could do that next time, but right now, he needed to show her how precious she was to him.

"*Ohh...*"

Working his way back up, he used his tongue to tease the corners of her mouth before slipping inside again. He took his time tasting, teasing, then transferred his kisses back to her throat. He paused briefly to remove her clothes, touching and caressing each part of her body as he went.

"I think I should have a chance to touch and kiss you, too," Nzinga said, coming up on her knees. Her hand immediately went to his belt. She never took her eyes off him as she undid his pants.

He arched up to help her remove them, then whipped his shirt over his head and tossed it aside. As her hand and mouth skated along his chest, abs and thighs, Byron grit his teeth to keep from exploding. At the first touch of her mouth on his engorged length, his body bucked and he swore hoarsely. After a few seconds, he stilled her.

"Problems?" she asked with a sultry smile.

"Big problems." Byron pulled her on top of him and lowered her onto his erection. She started an erotic swirl of her hips and he didn't think he was going to last a minute. His hands played over the curve of her hips, up her spine and around to her breasts, then slid back down to her hips as he plunged deeper. He leaned up and fused his mouth against hers. No other woman had come close to arousing the emotions in him she did. Her nails dug into his shoulders and her body tensed all around him. She let out another scream as she shuddered with her release. He tightened his hold on her hips, setting a rhythm with deep, powerful thrusts and came right behind her, growling loudly as an orgasm ripped through him with a force that rocked his soul. Nzinga collapsed on top of him, and he could feel her rapidly beating heart against his. The only sounds in the room were their ragged breathing.

"I think I like the way you touch and kiss me."

Chuckling, he said, "Ditto, baby." Their breathing slowed, hers deep and even. He tilted his head and saw she had fallen asleep on top of him. Byron smiled and tightened his arms around her. He'd been given a second chance, and he vowed to love her now and forever.

EPILOGUE

*O*ne *month later*
"You look so beautiful, Z," Donna said.

Nzinga stared at her reflection and had to agree. Her first thought had been to have a small wedding and wear a nice dress, but when Byron expressed how much he wanted to go all out, she couldn't deny his simple request. She loved him and wanted to make him as happy as he'd made her. Now, she stood wearing an ivory satin, off-the-shoulder floor-length wedding dress that flattered her figure. "I hope he likes it."

"Likes it? I hope he makes it through the wedding without dragging you off."

She shared a look with Max, recalling their conversation.

Val hugged her shoulders. "Be happy, sis."

"I am." She met each of her friend's gazes. "Thank you for being the sisters of my heart. I don't think I could've gotten through this life without you."

"Don't make us start crying before the wedding even starts," Val said.

Nzinga dabbed at the corners of her eyes, being careful not to smudge her makeup. "I know, I know."

Donna peeked out the door. "I think it's time."

"Okay." They all gave her a sisterly hug before departing. She took a deep breath and went out to where her father stood outside the door. "I'm ready, Dad."

Isaac Carlyle patted her cheek. "You're a beautiful bride, baby girl. I talked with Byron last night and I'm proud to call him son."

She felt her emotions rise. "You don't know how much that means to me."

He smiled and extended his arm. "Let's go meet your groom."

When the doors opened and Nzinga saw Byron standing at the end of the aisle, tall and devastatingly handsome, it took everything in her not to run to him. As if he'd interpreted her thoughts, he smiled and tossed her a wink. Her father placed her hand in Byron's and a peace she'd never experienced came over her. They faced the minister and recited their vows.

When it came time for their first kiss as husband and wife, Byron said, "I love you, Mrs. Walker."

His lips touched hers and, just like their first sweet kiss, she knew they were always meant to be.

ABOUT THE AUTHOR

Sheryl Lister is a multi-award-winning author and has enjoyed reading and writing for as long as she can remember. She is a former pediatric occupational therapist with over twenty years of experience, and resides in California. Sheryl is a wife, mother of three daughters and a son-in-love, and grandmother to two special little boys. When she's not writing, Sheryl can be found on a date with her husband or in the kitchen creating appetizers. For more information, visit her website at www.sheryllister.com.

ALSO BY SHERYL LISTER

HARLEQUIN KIMANI

Just To Be With You

All Of Me

It's Only You

Be Mine For Christmas (Unwrapping The Holidays Anthology)

Tender Kisses (The Grays of Los Angeles #1)

Places In My Heart (The Grays of Los Angeles #2)

Giving My All To You (The Grays of Los Angeles #3)

A Touch Of Love (The Grays of Los Angeles #4)

Still Loving You (The Grays of Los Angeles #5)

His Los Angeles Surprise

A Love Of My Own (The Hunters Of Sacramento #1)

Sweet Love (The Hunters Of Sacramento #2)

Spark Of Desire (The Hunters Of Sacramento #3)

Designed By Love (The Hunters Of Sacramento #4)

OTHER TITLES

Made To Love You

It's You That I Need

Perfect Chemistry

Embracing Forever (Once Upon A Bridesmaid #3)

Love's Serenade (Decades: A Journey Of African American

Romance #3)

Sweet Summer Days

The Reluctant Bid

Closer To You

Her Passionate Promise